A Flair for Truffles

A Flair for Truffles

A Sadie Kramer Flair Mystery

DEBORAH GARNER

CRANBERRY COVE PRESS

A Flair for Truffles
by Deborah Garner

First Printing – February 2019
ISBN: 978-0-9969961-2-9

Printed in the U.S.A.

*For all those who love chocolate, mystery,
and adventure—or any combination of the above.*

Books by Deborah Garner

The Paige MacKenzie Mystery Series

Above the Bridge
The Moonglow Café
Three Silver Doves
Hutchins Creek Cache
Crazy Fox Ranch

The Moonglow Christmas Novella Series

Mistletoe at Moonglow
Silver Bells at Moonglow
Gingerbread at Moonglow
Nutcracker Sweets at Moonglow
Snowfall at Moonglow

The Sadie Kramer Flair Series

A Flair for Chardonnay
A Flair for Drama
A Flair for Beignets
A Flair for Truffles
A Flair for Flip-Flops

Cranberry Bluff

ONE

Sadie looked over the assortment of chocolates and wondered how she'd ever decide which to try first. The combination Matteo had put together for his Valentine's Day special was nothing short of sinful.

"You've outdone yourself this time, Matteo," Sadie said, unable to take her eyes off the silky heart-shaped box of confections. "You always have a knack for unique chocolate treats, but this year's truffle extravaganza tops everything."

Matteo smiled at his most loyal customer. Sadie's fashion boutique, Flair, flanked his chocolate shop, Cioccolato, allowing the businesses to share customers. And Sadie's near addiction to chocolate made her the perfect taste-tester. Naturally, she generously offered her services whenever needed, as well as sometimes when not.

"I especially love the look of that one with the caramel drizzle on top," Sadie said as she continued to admire the assortment.

"Would you like to try it?" Matteo suggested, pulling a tray out from under the display counter.

"Why, yes! That would be delightful!" Sadie exclaimed, as if the thought had never crossed her mind.

Matteo lifted a truffle with a square of wax paper and held it out. Sadie grabbed it eagerly and popped it into her mouth. She closed her eyes and sighed. "Mm. Coffee," she mumbled. She placed one hand over her mouth as she let the delicious confection melt slowly.

"Caramel espresso to be exact," Matteo said.

"Yes, of course," Sadie said once she could speak clearly again. "That should sell well. In fact, the whole assortment will. I'm sure you'll be swamped today." Sadie glanced at the front door, noting several customers already outside. She felt privileged to be able to visit with Matteo before he opened for the day. Not only was it fun to chitchat with her handsome, Italian thirty-something neighbor, but it let her pick up samples for her own customers.

"Swamped is putting it mildly," Matteo said. He nodded toward a stack of boxes on the counter behind him. "I have to get those special orders out too. And I don't have anyone coming in until this afternoon to help."

"Ah, yes. Thanks for the reminder," Sadie said. "I have a delivery today too. Sue Bennett ordered a pink ruffled blouse to wear to a dinner event later this week. I told her I'd drop it by."

"Really?" Matteo looked up from the display case, his brown eyes matching the color of the dark-chocolate-raspberry truffles he was placing in neat rows. "I have a special order going to her today as well. Three, to be exact."

"Three?" Sadie eyed the stack of red boxes on the back counter. "Lucky woman. Someone must be feeling quite generous." Sadie couldn't help but be envious. To receive not one, not two, but three boxes of Matteo's creations would be heavenly.

"I'd say three people were feeling generous," Matteo said. "The orders all came from different customers."

"Really," Sadie said, even more impressed. Then again, Sue's friends had to know she loved chocolate as much—well, almost as much—as Sadie. No one could love chocolate as much as Sadie did. But Sue always grabbed a free sample or two when she came to check out Sadie's new clothing and accessory arrivals. And she almost always headed next door to buy some after she finished her purchases at Flair.

"Listen, Matteo," Sadie said. "I know you'll be going crazy today with all the sales for Valentine's Day. It's not as busy next door, and I have Amber to help. Why don't I just deliver those boxes to Sue Bennett when I take her the blouse she ordered?"

Matteo looked out the front window at the growing line. "I hate to ask a favor, but maybe I should take you up on that offer. It doesn't look like I'll have a minute to spare after I open up."

"That's a good problem to have in business," Sadie pointed out.

Matteo picked up the three boxes and started to hand them to Sadie, then pulled them back teasingly right before she grabbed them. "These *are* going to make it to Sue Bennett's house, right?"

Sadie laughed. "As if I don't know where to go for chocolate when I need it? Yes, of course. I'll deliver them to her personally."

"That's why I'm worried." Matteo winked as he placed the boxes in Sadie's hands.

Thanking Matteo for the extraordinary trust he was placing in her, Sadie returned to her boutique. Amber, her shop manager, was half-in and half-out of the front window display.

"Rearranging the window?" Sadie asked. She headed straight for the register counter where Coco sat on a velvet pillow. It was the perfect spot for her sidekick to spend time on shop days. Sadie always knew where she was, and the caramel-colored Yorkie received mounds of attention from customers.

"Just replacing a scarf." Amber's voice was muffled but

grew clearer as she backed out of the display. "Mrs. Wiggins wanted that red paisley scarf on the mannequin. We only had purple and green left on the rack, so I had to pull the one in the window and replace it with another." She straightened up and stretched her neck to one side, then the other.

"I'm so glad I have you to crawl around in that window most of the time," Sadie said. "I know that feeling of cramped neck and shoulder muscles, even without your lovely height in my genetic makeup."

"You know I don't mind," Amber said. "No point in taking all those yoga classes if I can't fold myself into a pretzel to arrange the front window!" Her eyebrows lifted as she eyed the boxes in Sadie's hands. "For us?"

Sadie shook her head. "Don't we wish! No, these are for Sue Bennett. I told Matteo I'd drop them off. We have a blouse to deliver to her anyway."

Amber nodded as she stepped behind the sales counter. "Yes, she called right before closing yesterday to see if it had come in. She's looking forward to wearing it for some sort of Valentine's Day event. I told her it had just arrived in the UPS delivery. She said her car will be in the shop for a couple of days and you offered to drop the blouse off."

"Yes, I did," Sadie said. "She wants to wear it to a special event tonight. Speaking of the UPS delivery…" Sadie grinned as she waited for Amber to respond. Amber's crush on the driver had been a subject of discussion for months. Sadie had encouraged her to ask him out on a date, stating that modern times allowed women as much right as men to instigate a lunch or dinner on the town.

"You're going to tease me about Dylan again, aren't you?" Amber blushed and busied herself rearranging a small tray of earrings on the counter.

Sadie placed her hand on Amber's to stop the young store manager from fidgeting. "You know this crush of yours isn't one-sided."

"You don't know that for sure," Amber said.

"Oh, I think I do." Sadie smiled, remembering her youthful days of flirting and being flirted with. "He takes his time when dropping off packages, always asking how you are." She released Amber's hand and patted Coco's head.

"He's very polite," Amber offered as she resumed arranging the earrings.

"And he often stops by on his lunch hour to see if we have any packages to go out," Sadie added. "You know we rarely ship anything, and when we do, we put a sign in the window."

Sadie watched as Amber silently fished for a rebuttal, coming up empty. "You know, romance is in the air this time of year." She lifted a pair of heart earrings, held them up on either side of Coco's head just for amusement, then put them back in the display.

"Sue Bennett's blouse is in the back, ready to go," Amber hinted, looking grateful for an excuse to change the subject. Sadie let her get away with it, knowing she teased the girl enough, if not too much.

"Yes," Sadie said. "And I'd better deliver it before we get tempted to break into her boxes from Matteo's."

"We?" Amber laughed.

"Okay, you've got me there," Sadie said. "Before I get tempted to break into them. Of course, we could always buy another to replace one…" Her voice trailed off.

"Sadie…," Amber prompted.

"Just kidding," Sadie said. "Sort of," she added, laughing as she added the customer's blouse delivery to the boxes of chocolates and grabbed her tote bag from the back office. She placed Coco comfortably in the tote, bid Amber goodbye, and headed off to Sue Bennett's house.

TWO

Sadie glanced at her GPS as she waited at a red traffic light. She'd never been to Sue Bennett's home but had ordered items to be drop-shipped directly from vendors, so she'd had the address even before offering to deliver the blouse. The woman lived in the posh San Francisco neighborhood of Russian Hill on Lombard Street. It wouldn't be hard to find.

The light turned green, and Sadie continued on. She knew the area well enough to expect a refined, immaculately restored Victorian house on a quiet block with peaceful surroundings. What she found when she arrived was anything but that.

"Oh dear!" Sadie exclaimed. "This doesn't look good at all, Coco." The Yorkie stuck her head out of the tote and looked around. Too short to see above the dashboard, the petite canine sighed and dropped back inside the bag.

Pulling over to the curb, Sadie turned off the ignition and took in the scene. Multiple police cars surrounded one stately home, which was painted in pastel colors with gingerbread-style trim around the eaves. Yellow tape blocked off the property, and clusters of neighbors stood on the sidewalks, conversing with each other and watching the activity around the house.

Sadie left Coco in her tote bag and exited the vehicle, boxes of chocolates in her arms. Fairly certain she wasn't going to be able to deliver them now, she still wasn't going to risk leaving them near Coco. Any responsible pet owner knew that dogs and chocolate did not mix.

Approaching the others on the sidewalk, Sadie found a spot where she could both watch and overhear discussions. Certainly, eavesdropping was justified occasionally.

"I just knew it would come down to something like this," a woman said. The shapely, middle-aged woman was holding a broom and seemed to be directing her comments to anyone and everyone. She wore a housecoat, and her salt-and-pepper hair was in disarray. "Different men coming and going from her house, for one thing, and that crazy work schedule." She clucked her tongue.

"Mags," another neighbor said. "She was a flight attendant, for heaven's sake. Of *course* she had a crazy work schedule."

The woman named Mags let out a huff. "Well, it seemed strange to me." Sadie noticed more than one neighbor roll their eyes. Clearly, Mags was known for spouting her opinions, not to mention keeping an eye on the neighborhood. As if to prove Sadie's point, the woman spotted her and called over. "And who are you? I haven't seen you around here before."

Sadie offered her name and her reason for being there, though it seemed odd to be interrogated simply because she'd come by to drop off a few deliveries. Still, an answer would be the best way to get the woman to back off. "I came to drop off something Sue Bennett ordered from my store, as well as chocolate assortments from Cioccolato."

"Well, I'll be happy to take the chocolate off your hands," Mags offered. "Everything that shop sells is delicious."

First reasonable thing the woman has said, Sadie thought, not that she was about to hand the boxed truffles over. She could think of better solutions if Matteo couldn't take them back. "A kind offer," Sadie said, trying to keep her sarcasm under wraps. "But I'll need to take them back to the shop since it seems I'll be unable to deliver them. What happened anyway?"

"I'll tell you what I think…," Mags began. "I think it was one of those men she'd been seeing. Maybe the skinny, sleazy one who slinked around like a weasel. Yep, I bet he did it."

"Did what?" Sadie asked, already trying to get the description of the man out of her mind.

"Killed her, that's what," Mags said. "Why do you think the place is taped off? Besides, look who's pulling up." Sadie followed Mags's arm gesture. Sure enough, the coroner's vehicle had just arrived.

Mags turned away from Sadie to another woman standing nearby. "Don't you think so, Linda? That slinky guy must have killed her. I mean, he seemed the type. Not trustworthy."

The woman Mags addressed as Linda shot Mags a dubious look. "You didn't even know the guy. You can't just go around accusing people of something serious, especially without knowing them."

"Well, I just didn't like the way he looked." Mags crossed her arms as if to solidify her point. "And I saw him plenty of times."

"Of course you did," Linda said. "From that front window of yours. Don't you have better things to do than watch the neighborhood all the time?"

Mags shrugged her shoulders. "Someone has to."

"You're like that character in the old show," Linda said. "The one about the witch who could wiggle her nose and her house would be clean. I always wanted to be able to pull that off. What was that show called?"

"*Bewitched*," Sadie said.

"Yes, that one. Thank you." Linda turned away to talk to

other neighbors, but Mags continued to hover near Sadie.

"Who are the chocolates from? Looks like you have three boxes," Mags leaned forward in an obvious attempt to read the name on the top box.

"I don't know," Sadie said, moving the boxes away from the woman's intruding gaze. "I just offered to drop them off. It's not really any of my business." *Or yours*, Sadie added silently.

The conversation paused as two police officers stepped out of the Victorian house. They descended the front steps and began questioning observers on the sidewalk. Mags abruptly turned away from Sadie and rushed over to offer whatever information she knew and likely some she didn't. Sadie took advantage of the moment to walk back to her car. As she opened the door, her cell phone rang. She set the boxes of chocolate down and reached into a side pocket of her tote bag to pull the phone out. Coco let out a small yip of protest at being disturbed.

"Hi, Amber," Sadie said, having recognized the phone number for the store. She slid into the driver's seat and listened to Amber recount a customer request. "Yes, we can order that sweater in for Mrs. Figtree. Just write down the color and size she needs. It comes in pastel blue, yellow and pink, I believe. ... Maybe in lavender, I'll have to check. I'll be back shortly." ... "No, I wasn't able to. It turns out I won't be delivering the blouse or the chocolates, I'm afraid. I'll explain when I get back."

Sadie disconnected the call and slipped the cell phone back in the tote's pocket. From a separate pocket, she pulled out a bone-shaped treat and dropped it into the bag. Smiling at the soft crunching that followed, she watched Mags move from one officer to the other, trying to peek at their notepads. Her arms flew about in exaggerated gestures. The officers appeared to be listening politely while trying to give equal attention to other neighbors.

"Quite a scene," Sadie said, shaking her head. "And poor Ms. Bennett. I didn't really know her, but you liked her, Coco. She always took time to pet you when she came into the shop." Coco's head popped up above the rim of the tote at the sound of her name. Sadie gave Coco a pat on the head and then started the car. "Let's go, Coco. We'd better get back to the shop and give Matteo the news."

THREE

Sadie bit into a mocha-caramel truffle and watched Matteo set the boxes of chocolates down behind the counter.

"Well, that's a first," Matteo said. "And hopefully a last. What a horrible reason for someone not to receive chocolates they'd been sent. I've had deliveries get crushed, get lost, get stolen, even melt before they reached their destination, but never returned because the intended recipient wasn't alive to receive them. It's terrible."

"Yes, it is," Sadie agreed. "And one of the neighbors seemed quite convinced it wasn't from natural causes."

"Murder?" Matteo's eyebrows lifted in surprise. He offered Sadie another truffle, which she readily accepted.

"That's what Gladys Kravitz thinks." Sadie popped the chocolate into her mouth as she contemplated the odd behavior of Sue Bennett's neighbor.

"Who?" Matteo asked.

"A character from a television show back in the '60s," Sadie said. "You're too young to remember it." In truth, Sadie wasn't quite sure how old Matteo was, but he was definitely not out of his thirties yet. He was from the *Cheers* and *MacGyver* generation.

"Ah, a busybody," Matteo said as he slid a tray of maple-nut fudge into the display case. "I wouldn't take her word for it. The woman probably died of natural causes."

"Maybe," Sadie admitted. "But Gla—I mean—Mags was talking about different men coming and going, including one she referred to as 'skinny and slinky.'"

"Not very complimentary," Matteo noted.

"No, not at all," Sadie said. "Does he match the description of any of the three who ordered chocolates for her?"

Matteo shrugged. "I have no idea. They were all phone orders."

"Did any of them have a skinny, slinky voice?" Sadie laughed as soon as the words left her mouth, knowing the question was ridiculous. Voices over the phone might conjure up an image, but it was purely imagined until seeing the person. She'd spoken with many customers who called in to inquire about availability of an item, only to find they looked entirely different from her imagined perception when they showed up to shop.

"One did sound a little weird, now that I think about it," Matteo said. "But that's hardly a reason to suspect he's a killer. *If* there is a killer at all. You don't know that."

"True," Sadie admitted.

"Maybe your inner amateur detective is showing a little. You sure you want to get involved with this?"

"Well, I was at the scene," Sadie offered as an excuse. "Besides, we're in possession of information that could be of use to the police."

Matteo looked at Sadie. "How so?"

"You have three leads," Sadie pointed out. "Three people who sent Sue Bennett chocolate. You should turn that information over to the police."

"And bother innocent people who probably have nothing to do with this?" Matteo shook his head. "No, it is bad enough I'm going to have to tell them their orders couldn't be delivered. Speaking of which, I'd better call them and run their refunds."

The door chimed, and a mother and young girl entered. The child, who looked to be around six years of age, skipped directly to the display case and pressed her face against the glass, hands splayed to each side.

Sadie returned to Flair so Matteo could deal with customers and make the necessary calls. She placed Coco on the Yorkie's store pillow and filled Amber in on the details she knew, few as they were.

"Maybe your new detective friend can get you some inside information," Amber suggested, a sly smile on her slender, oval face.

Sadie started to protest but stopped. Fair was fair. She teased Amber about the UPS guy. Amber certainly had a right to respond in kind. And Sadie *had* taken a liking to the detective she'd met on a recent trip to New Orleans. It did feel odd to have a flirtation going on, but Morris, her husband, had been gone for years.

"It's not exactly in his jurisdiction, you know," Sadie quipped, fighting back a smile.

"It could be a crime that matches another crime in his area," Amber countered. "Then he could call and compare details. That could help solve a case in New Orleans."

Sadie shook her head. "First, how many episodes of CSI have you been watching recently? And second, we don't even know if it's a crime or not."

Amber turned her attention to a woman approaching the register to make a purchase. The customer wore a glossy raincoat and sported a heavy layer of makeup. She gave Coco a dubious stare as she set a silk scarf on the counter and pushed it away from the pillow.

"Don't worry," Sadie offered lightly, trying to elicit a smile from the dour woman. "She doesn't eat scarves." Earning the same look that Coco had received, Sadie tried to come up with a different comment, but Coco beat her to it, voicing a short yip of objection to the woman's attitude. "Coco! Be polite. I think you may just need a time out."

Excusing herself, Sadie lifted Coco and the pillow and moved to the back office, taking a seat and getting Coco situated on top of her desk. She couldn't blame the petite canine for reacting. Dogs had a unique perception about people, and the customer *had seemed* off-putting. Still, Sadie hadn't recognized the woman, so she was likely a new customer. New customers only became repeat customers if they enjoyed their shopping experience. Maybe having Coco out of the way would let Amber pacify the woman while ringing up her scarf. A little extra tissue paper, perhaps, and a sample truffle—that often helped.

Amber appeared in the office doorway a minute later. She shrugged her shoulders. "Not a word of thanks."

"We can't please everyone," Sadie said. "All we can do is try our best. There will always be a random person here or there who won't be satisfied, no matter what. It's likely the person's general demeanor other places, as well. We can't take it personally."

"That's a sad way to go through life," Amber said as she backed out of the door to return to the front counter.

"Indeed," Sadie muttered to herself and then patted Coco on the head. "If only everyone had your bright outlook on life." Coco tilted her head to the side, pleased with the attention even if oblivious to the exact compliment.

An incoming call on her cell phone interrupted Sadie's thought process. She fished it out of her tote bag and answered cautiously, seeing that the screen flashed No Caller ID.

"Hello?"

"Is this Sadie Kramer?" The man's voice was unfamiliar and serious.

"Yes, it is," Sadie said. "How may I help you?"

"This is Detective Frogert of SFPD. I just have a few questions for you."

Sadie was immediately struck by two entirely separate thoughts. One: Whoever this detective was, she would end up calling him "Froggy," even if not to his face. And two: Why was he calling, and how on earth did he get her phone number?"

"Yes, Detective," Sadie said. "May I ask why you're calling me?" She wasn't about to give out any information if this was a prank call. Based on his name, it could have been. Then again, who would use such a ridiculous fake name if he didn't need to?

"I'm investigating a crime on Lombard Street."

Sadie almost dropped the phone. *This is what I get for volunteering to deliver chocolate?* "I'm sorry, but I still don't understand why you're calling or why you have my phone number."

"Your car was observed at the scene," the detective said. "Your license plate was reported by…" A shuffling of papers followed. "…by a Margaret Gabston."

Sadie snorted. "Of *course* her name would be Gabster." *Mags. Gabs for short. It has a nice ring to it.*

"Gabston, ma'am," the detective corrected, his voice impatient.

"Yes, of course," Sadie said. "I can explain."

"That would be most helpful."

"You know that Valentine's Day is coming up, right?" Sadie

asked, feeling it important to provide general background information.

"My wife reminds me daily," the detective said, his voice monotone. "Continue, please."

"I offered to deliver three boxes of chocolates for my neighbor, Matteo. He owns Cioccolato, a fabulous chocolate shop. Perhaps you've heard of it?" Sadie paused to wait for an answer. No harm in doing a little advertising on Matteo's behalf. "It's a wonderful place to pick up chocolate for a gift."

"My wife reminds me of that too."

"I see," Sadie said. "Well, it's quite simple. The chocolate boxes were for Sue Bennett, as well as a blouse she had ordered from my boutique, Flair. Perhaps your wife…" Deciding not to push her luck, Sadie quickly added, "Anyway, I went to deliver everything and saw the commotion, so I left. That's really the whole story, at least as much as I know."

"And where are the chocolate boxes now?" More paper shuffling.

"I returned them to Matteo's shop when I couldn't deliver them, of course," Sadie said, frowning. "Why?" *Sheesh, buy your own chocolate!* What kind of a deadbeat husband was this guy anyway?

"Thank you, Ms. Kramer," the detective said. "That'll be all for now. I'll be in touch."

The line disconnected, leaving Sadie with an uneasy feeling. Talk about being in the wrong place at the wrong time.

"Nothing to worry about, Coco," Sadie said, noticing Coco had tensed up during the phone call, a reaction to Sadie's annoyed tone. "I'm sure Froggy can figure this one out without our help."

FOUR

"Matteo," Sadie said as she leaned across Cioccolato's front counter, "I need to find out who was sending Sue Bennett those boxes."

Matteo, as she expected, hesitated. "You wouldn't give out customer information, Sadie, even to me. At least not without good reason."

"I would if you were a person of interest in a crime," Sadie said.

"And you think you are?" Matteo gave Sadie a dubious look. Sadie merely admired a row of coconut almond clusters he was arranging, almost forgetting her quest.

"I know I am," Sadie said, focusing her attention back on the chocolatier. "Froggy practically said so."

"Froggy? You've lost me now," Matteo said, moving on to touch up a display of caramels.

"Detective Frogert from SFPD called to question me. It seems that annoying woman at the scene took down my license plate and gave it to the police."

"Really?" Matteo's eyebrows lifted. "I see you weren't exaggerating about her being a busybody. It seems extreme to involve you. You were only there to make a delivery."

"You know that, and I know that, but apparently the police don't know that." Sadie sighed. Just verbalizing the situation made it sound more absurd. "So you see, these are extenuating circumstances. Besides, there's a good chance your customers are also my customers. That's usually true."

"You make a good case," Matteo said. "Maybe you should have gone into law."

The front door chimed as a trio of men entered. Sadie eyed them all suspiciously, which caused Matteo to shake his head in amusement. Grabbing a clipboard of orders from a back wall, he slid it over a side counter and turned his attention to the new customers.

Sadie grabbed the order sheets eagerly and took the liberty of slipping out the door while Matteo was occupied. *Ten minutes with this next door can't hurt, can it?*

Back at her boutique, she waved the clipboard at Amber and hustled through the shop to her back office. Seated at her desk, she flipped through the orders, soon identifying the three that were intended for Sue Bennett. *The victim*, Sadie thought, redefining the poor woman's status. The detective had called it a crime, so there was no question now.

Was it a crime of passion maybe? Valentine's Day chocolate orders often indicated romance. Sadie mulled it over, remembering a time when a doting aunt had sent her chocolate. So romance was not necessarily in the cards here, but it was a reasonable place to start. And start she would. For one thing, she needed ammunition in case the police pushed her further. For another, she never could resist a good mystery. Besides, didn't she owe it to Sue Bennett to get to the bottom of this? She hadn't really known the woman personally, but she'd been a decent customer over the years. She could always be counted on to show up for the yearly clearance sale. Yes, Sadie had plenty of good reasons to investigate.

"I just sold that lavender dress with the lace collar and ruffled skirt," Amber said. "Mrs. Simpson plans to wear it to church on Easter. And... might I ask what you're up to now? I sense one of your adventures coming on."

"You have the keenest intuition," Sadie said, smiling. Amber had managed Flair for years and was well aware of Sadie's penchant for amateur detective challenges.

"Don't get yourself in trouble," Amber warned. Her tone was more kind than intrusive.

Sadie sat back and sighed. "I'm afraid I already am."

Amber glanced behind her to make sure no new customers had entered and then looked back at Sadie, confused. "How is that possible?"

"You wouldn't think it would be, but I've already had a call from the police," Sadie explained. "Some detective named Froggy, who said my license plate was noted at the scene."

"Froggy?" Amber fought back a youthful smile.

"Detective Frogert, to be precise. But he deserves the nickname. I mean, who names a child like that?" Sadie had started perusing the orders and spoke absentmindedly.

Amber laughed. "I believe people give their children first names, not last."

Sadie looked up, lost in thought. "All three chocolate orders were from men."

"That's typical for this time of year," Amber said. "Don't you think?"

"You mean romance? Such as you might have if you asked Dylan out?"

Amber tilted her head and eyed Sadie pointedly. "Speaking of romance, have you heard from your New Orleans detective?" Amber crossed her arms and smirked. Coco, curled up on Sadie's desk, seemed to mimic Amber's expression.

"Not recently," Sadie said, trying to ignore the fact that Amber had issued the perfect rebuttal to Sadie's teasing comment.

"Well, it seems you have a perfect excuse to contact him," Amber said. "Not that you need one. You know he's interested. Didn't I see you sneak a delivery of flowers out of here shortly after you returned from New Orleans?" Coco now eyed Sadie with a look that seemed almost accusatory.

Amber had a point. All Sadie could do was plead the fifth. She shrugged her shoulders.

The sound of the bell over the shop's front door saved Sadie from additional prodding, but Amber did toss one more comment over her shoulder as she turned to head back into the store to greet customers. "Long distance calls are included on your cell phone plan…"

"There's no reason to double team me," Sadie said, giving Coco a playful pat on the head. "I saw you agreeing with her."

Sadie listened to the muffled voices of boutique commerce floating back from the front of the store. A call to Detective Broussard in New Orleans could be helpful. John—*Jean-Pierre*, technically—had experience handling this type of situation. Undoubtedly, he wouldn't be pleased to know her license plate was noted at the scene. Not because it had brought the police to her door, figuratively speaking, but because he'd know she'd be unable to resist nosing into the situation. And even Sadie knew some things were better off left alone.

Pushing all those thoughts out of her mind, including the flutters she felt at the idea of talking to Broussard, she turned her attention back to the order forms from the three men who'd ordered the chocolates for Sue Bennett. She ran copies on the office printer, then rearranged the papers on the clipboard so she could return it to Matteo. With his shop busy with customers, she could simply slide the batch of orders back on the side counter before heading out to do some innocent snooping around.

FIVE

The Stannon-Fielder building stood a good twenty stories high, its modern glass and metal siding gleaming as a few rays of sunlight made their way through the common San Francisco fog. The Montgomery Street location placed it smack in the middle of the city's Financial District, a predictable place to find the first of the three men Sadie sought. Luke Manning, like Sadie's late husband, Morris, dabbled in real estate investments. It hadn't taken but a few searches on her computer to track him down. Conveniently, he'd used his business phone number on the chocolate order.

"Can I help you, ma'am?" a gentleman asked as he emerged through the front door. He wore a business suit that likely cost more than Flair took in during the course of a week. Relatively handsome and in his forties, he was clearly rushing. Sadie was impressed that he'd taken the time to ask if she needed assistance. Few people seemed to do that these days.

"Just admiring the building," Sadie said, craning her neck upward. "It's very tall." *It's very tall? That's my best small talk for the moment?* Still, she was on the prowl, so to speak, and not eager to get into a conversation. She was already in a mess simply from standing on a sidewalk earlier that morning.

"Yes, it is," the man said, obviously for lack of a better response. "Good day then." He hurried off to whatever appointment he must have had, disappearing into a nearby parking garage with a FULL sign posted at its entryway.

Grateful she'd managed to find a parking place on the street—a rare find indeed in San Francisco—she turned back to the building.

Sadie continued to look up until her neck and shoulders began to ache, then lowered her gaze to the front entrance. The revolving door served to beckon her inside, and she soon found herself in the lobby, looking at a directory on the wall.

Manning Property Holdings was situated on the seventeenth floor, an impressive location that was sure to have a spectacular view of the bay. That their offices encompassed the entire floor told her the company was likely successful and Luke Manning even more likely to be—to put it delicately— filthy rich.

Being wealthy wasn't a crime in itself, and it stood to reason that people of any financial status might be capable of murder. It was truly an equal opportunity crime in many aspects. But it probably ruled out one motive: money. Sue Bennett lived— make that had lived—in a ritzy neighborhood. She must have had a few dollars stashed away. *Come to think of it, she did always scout the sales racks…* Sadie brushed the ridiculous thought away. The point was, Luke Manning's portfolio was surely plumper than Sue Bennett's.

Had the deceased been a client of Manning Property Holdings? A disgruntled client? A content client with a disgruntled financial manager? Had a deal headed south, leaving ill feelings on the side of both parties? Or *multiple* parties?

Sadie took a seat on a bench in the foyer, setting her tote bag beside her. "What do you think, Coco?" Coco stuck her head out of the bag at the sound of her name. "Plenty of possibilities here, don't you think? And we haven't even checked the other two names out yet." Always one to back

Sadie up, Coco yipped in agreement.

"It's really not appropriate to bring dogs into public buildings if they can't keep quiet."

Sadie glanced up to see an extravagantly dressed woman pressing the Up button for the elevator. The combination of silk, cashmere, and pearls struck Sadie as heavy overkill for daytime wear. And the rock on the ring finger of the woman's left hand was ostentatious.

She does look elegant, Sadie thought as she observed the woman's refined demeanor. *I'll bet her name is something like Juliette or maybe Anastasia...*

The woman glanced at Sadie briefly, dismissing her as if she were some sort of eccentric senior citizen who carried a dog around in a tote bag!

Oh wait, Sadie thought. I *am* an eccentric senior citizen who carries a dog around in a tote bag.

As far as Sadie was concerned, she had plenty of class without having to flash it around. She had a style all her own. She might prefer a bright chunky necklace of plastic beads to a string of pearls, but she didn't feel a need to dress to impress. Morris had left her with a hefty portfolio and a penthouse apartment. Looks could be deceiving.

The thought came right back to smack her in the conscience. The woman, who thankfully had now stepped into the elevator and started on her upward journey, could be wearing her only decent outfit. And the hefty, sparkling rock could be cubic zirconium. Who could even tell the difference these days?

Coco yipped as if to chastise Sadie for her temporary pettiness.

"You're right, Coco," Sadie said. "I'm not setting a very good example for you." She looked back at the elevator the woman had taken, noticing it had stopped on the seventeenth floor. "Well, now that's interesting," she said to Coco. "I see all kinds of possibilities here." *For example, a ring that size could be a weapon.*

Realizing her imagination was starting to get the better of her, Sadie picked up her tote bag, precious contents and all, and stepped over to the elevator. A quick visit to Manning Property Holdings wouldn't take long. She'd ask if Luke Manning was available, citing a money market account that she was contemplating liquidating for a real estate purchase. Asking for a consultation was a simple excuse for visiting a financial company. She had no appointment, so didn't expect to be seen. But it would give her a chance to look around.

A few minutes later, Sadie stepped out of the elevator and into a marble-tiled lobby, elegant yet sparsely decorated, with a sole receptionist sitting behind a mahogany desk. There was no sign of the woman who'd first taken the elevator.

"I'm wondering if it might be possible to see Mr. Manning," Sadie said.

The receptionist, an attractive woman in her thirties, looked up and responded politely. "I'm afraid he just stepped out. Did you have an appointment?"

"No, I didn't," Sadie said, feigning an apologetic tone. "I was just passing by, so I thought I'd stop in. He was recommended to me by my accountant."

"I see." The woman nodded and turned to her computer screen. "Mr. Manning's upcoming calendar is full, but perhaps you'd like to make an appointment with one of the junior associates?"

"Let me check my schedule," Sadie said. She pulled her cell phone out of a side pocket on her tote and tapped the keys. With the phone facing away from the reception desk, there was no way the woman would know she was merely tapping random icons. "It looks like I'll need to check my commitments back at my office," she said, putting the cell phone away.

"Perhaps you'd like to leave a message? Your name and phone number?" The receptionist picked up a pen and poised it over a notepad.

"That's all right," Sadie said. "I'll just call back." She took a business card from a holder on the desk and waved it in the air. Thanking the woman, she returned to the elevator and then to the first floor. Exiting the building, she headed back to her car, where, to her surprise, she found a man leaning against it.

"Ms. Kramer." The man, dressed in slacks and a jacket, but no tie, appeared to be in his forties. With a hairline that was receding and a waistline that was expanding, he resembled a shoe salesman or a car dealer, perhaps. But his badge gave him away.

"Detective Frogert," Sadie said. "Are you following me?" Coco, hearing the tension in Sadie's voice, stuck her head out of the tote and eyed the man.

"I didn't think I was," Detective Frogert said. "I was coming by to see someone in the Stannon-Fielder building and just happened to notice this license plate." He nodded toward the front of her car. "It seemed familiar. Quite a coincidence, don't you think?"

"Coincidences happen every day," Sadie offered for lack of anything else to say.

"Why don't we cut to the chase?" Detective Frogert pushed himself away from the car and took on a serious tone. "You were at Manning Property Holdings just now, is that correct?"

"That's not a crime," Sadie said, feeling defensive. "It's a public building. It's not like I was trespassing."

"No, but it's the second time today you've been somewhere

of interest to me, so I need to ask you what you're doing here." The detective eyed Sadie suspiciously, which caused her to switch from feeling defensive to feeling annoyed.

"Detective Frogert," Sadie said as she took a step closer. "You called me today as if I had something to do with whatever happened to Sue Bennett. I don't even *know* what happened to her. I only know I couldn't deliver the chocolates I intended to drop off. I then returned to my store, fully intending to mind my own business."

"Yet here you are," Frogert pointed out.

"Yes, because you've now involved me," Sadie said. "It made me curious to see who had ordered the deliveries."

"Then I suggest you un-involve yourself," the detective said.

Not really my modus operandi, Sadie thought, knowing better than to say it out loud. She reached inside her tote bag and pretended to dig for her car keys. "Sure," she said, her fingers crossed. "Am I free to leave now?" She pulled her keys out and waved them in the air. A giant purple pom-pom dangled from the key chain.

"You were never detained," Frogert said. Standing back, he extended his arm toward her vehicle. "Be my guest. And may we not accidentally run into each other again."

Fine by me, Sadie said to herself. She hopped in the car and buckled her seat belt, as well as the harness she used to safely secure her tote bag and Coco. Waving to the detective with a forced smile, she pulled away from the curb and headed back to the store.

SIX

Sadie looked out the window of her penthouse, admiring the San Francisco night lights. She took a sip of her favorite chardonnay, content to be relaxing at home in comfy leopard-print loungewear. For a day that should have been routine, it had certainly gone in a strange direction. First the botched chocolate delivery, then the bizarre exchanges with the SFPD detective, not to mention the unfortunate demise of a valued customer. This was not the ordinary day she'd expected when she first woke up that morning.

"It strikes me as peculiar, Coco," Sadie said. "How is it that Froggy just happened to be outside Manning Property Holdings the same time I was?" She moved away from the window and took a seat on the couch. Coco, busy batting around her favorite red lobster toy, didn't respond. "Was he on his way to see Luke Manning, or was he simply following me?"

The last thought was particularly disturbing as it either meant he considered her a person of interest, or he was benefiting from her own detective work. Maybe it was just his attitude that bothered her, but at least he could do his own investigating. It wasn't like she was being paid to help the local law enforcement. And she certainly didn't need a detective pestering her for no good reason. Unless…

Well, of course it would be different if the detective in question were Broussard. She might be fine having him pester her a bit. Just a bit though. As a widow, she'd become used to her independence. She had her own habits, not to mention her own financial security, home, shop, and beloved companion, Coco. Still, the handsome detective had caught her interest. She heard from him at least once a week and sent him an email about as often, which is why it didn't seem out of the norm to send him a quick note.

Moving to her home computer, she fired it up and opened her email. She deleted several annoying spam notices and passed over miscellaneous requests for charity donations. She frequently gave to good causes, but this wasn't her mission for the evening. Instead, she composed an email to Broussard, detailing the events of the day. She included her run-in with Detective Froggy… er, Frogert, taking care to make it clear it was the man himself who annoyed her, not the involvement of law enforcement.

With the time difference between San Francisco and New Orleans, she didn't expect an immediate reply. Yet it was only ten minutes later that her cell phone rang. Sure enough, it was the detective—the one she *wasn't* annoyed with—calling.

"Detective Broussard," Sadie said, using her most professional voice. It was a teasing habit they'd carried on since meeting on official business.

"Ms. Kramer," Broussard responded. "An honor, as always, to receive your email, worrisome as this one may be."

Sadie took another sip of chardonnay, which she had almost forgotten about in her haste to compose the email. "I didn't mean to worry you but thought you might have some advice."

"Aside from staying out of the situation before you complicate things more than it sounds like they already are?"

While thinking of a rebuttal, she decided another sip of wine was in order. She gathered her thoughts quickly and responded, using care to not sound defensive. "I didn't choose to be in the middle of this. I went to deliver chocolates for Matteo—you really must try his almond-coconut clusters, they are remarkable—and left when I saw the house taped off."

"Meanwhile getting your license plate on file with SFPD."

"Yes, but that was because of Gladys," Sadie explained.

"I thought you said the customer's name was Sue Bennett. The victim is more accurate, I believe. Who is Gladys?"

"I meant Mags," Sadie said. "Mags is Gladys. Gladys isn't real. She's a fictional television character. She's the one who took down my license plate number."

There was silence on the line for a few seconds. "Don't be offended at this, but is there a chance you've been drinking?"

"Four sips over the course of an hour," Sadie said. It was accurate. The glass wasn't even half-empty. And no, she hadn't had one before the one she currently held in her hand.

"All right," Broussard said. "I'll give you the benefit of the doubt on this and assume it was the actual person named Mags who took down your license plate and gave it to the police. Not the fictional one, which would be problematic on several levels. Why would Mags do that?"

"Because that's just what Gladys does."

More silence. "Okay, we'll go with that," Broussard said. "I don't think you have anything to worry about. It's normal the detective would want to speak with people who were at the scene."

"Like on TV? They say guilty people might return to the scene of the crime." Sadie reprimanded herself silently for not paying more attention to the others who were watching from the sidewalk. "Come to think of it, however, I doubt they arrive bearing chocolates."

"Not everything resembles what you see on television." Broussard's voice held the telltale tone of someone trying not to laugh. He quickly became more serious. "My advice is probably not what you want to hear, but I strongly suggest you keep your distance. Obviously, that includes *not* chasing down potential suspects."

Sadie mentally kicked herself for mentioning her trip to Luke Manning's office in her email. She should have known it wouldn't go over well. Still, the fact that Detective Frogert had caught up with her there was disturbing. "I figured if I could clear myself, Froggy would leave me alone."

Again, silence. She should have predicted it this time. "Is this Froggy another fictional character, Sadie? You're starting to worry me."

"No, he's the detective," Sadie said. "And I'd like him to leave me alone." She could envision Broussard nodding on the other end of the line.

"That can be easily arranged," Broussard said. "All you have to do is…" Sadie suspected *mind your own business* to be the next words she'd hear. Instead, Broussard said, "Just stay away. Run your shop, eat chocolate, and let the detective do his job."

"You should also try Matteo's maple-pecan truffles," Sadie said, distracted by the mention of chocolate. "They're divine. Maybe I should send you some." The unintentional change of subject worked to her advantage, as the conversation turned to everyday topics, with a touch of light flirtation mixed in.

"Promise me you'll stay out of this," Broussard said before the call ended.

"I promise," Sadie said. Phone calls being what they were, she didn't even have to hide her hand in her tote bag to cross her fingers.

SEVEN

The boutique smelled faintly of roses when Sadie arrived the next morning. Amber was rubbing her slender hands together, rotating them at different angles in order to glide each hand over a different portion of the other.

"The garden rose hand lotion, I presume," Sadie said. She helped Coco get situated on the counter pillow and looked over a new display Amber had set up not far from the register. "Smart, putting out a tester. The shop will undoubtedly smell like a rose garden whenever customers try it, but that'll only add to the ambiance." Sadie pushed the pump on top of the sample bottle and rubbed some on her own hands. "I love the way you've added a red-and-pink-satin ribbon and a dangling red heart tag to the ones for sale too."

Amber smiled, pleased with the compliment. "It makes it a ready-to-go gift," she said. "It should be an easy upsell. Next I'm going to set up the spring sweater shelves, and then I'll rearrange the beaded jewelry in the display case, and then I thought…" She turned to a back counter, checking a long list of notes.

"Four or five cups today?" Sadie asked.

Amber turned back toward her. "You know me too well. Three here, plus the one I always pick up at Jay's Java Joint on the way over."

"Which I believe is a double espresso," Sadie said. "Do you have the decaf brewing in the back office yet?"

Amber nodded. "Already started it."

"Smart girl." Sadie laughed. "Maybe just choose three projects and spread them throughout the day. I suspect we'll be busy with last-minute Valentine purchases anyway. Only a couple more shopping days."

As Amber began giving Coco a good-morning mini-massage, Sadie walked back to her office. She turned on her computer and, while waiting for it to warm up, checked her phone messages. As usual, the few calls were from sales reps looking to show upcoming fashion items and accessories for late summer and early fall. It was always necessary to plan at least a season ahead of time. Sadie had already placed orders for the items Flair would carry through fall.

Turning her attention to the online issue of the *SF Chronicle*, Sadie skimmed the headlines. Upstaged in placement by a capsized boat and several tax initiatives, the article Sadie sought was linked in a side column. "Body of Woman Found in Russian Hill Home," the link read. Sadie clicked through to the short report of Sue Bennett's death. While not a source of additional information, it did confirm that the police suspected foul play. Although this was not news to Sadie, seeing it in print gave it a semblance of validity. As she had suspected, Sue Bennett had been murdered.

"Any news?" Amber asked, sticking her head inside the doorway. "About Sue Bennett?"

"Not really," Sadie said. "The paper online says the police suspect foul play, but I already assumed that. Froggy wouldn't have bothered tracking me down if she'd died of natural causes."

"Froggy?"

Sadie looked up at Amber and smiled. "Yes, a detective who contacted me yesterday."

"That must have been annoying," Amber said. She excused herself as she heard people entering the shop.

"Yes, very annoying. I'd say annoying is an understatement," Sadie said out loud to no one in particular since Amber had returned to the front of the store. The clicking of hangers and friendly chatter were the only sounds she heard.

Checking other news sources, Sadie still came up without additional tidbits of information, which only meant one thing: she'd need to keep snooping around herself. Having only the copies of the chocolate orders to work with, she pulled them out and flipped to one of the two she had yet to investigate.

Finding the name Zane Grey on the second order sheet caused Sadie to pause. The famous American author had died a good eighty years earlier, but the mental image of him standing at Matteo's counter placing an order still flitted through her head. She pushed it aside quickly, moving on to her next supposition. Perhaps this was a fake name for someone not wishing it known that he was ordering a gift. A married man, perhaps? Or someone with another girlfriend with jealous tendencies? She made a note to ask Matteo if the person had ordered chocolate for more than one recipient. Meanwhile, she'd go with a third option: that this particular Zane Grey was neither long dead nor using a pseudonym. It was possible that Zane Grey just might be his name.

The local printed phone directory—yes, she actually had one—proved useless. Aside from being half-filled with advertising, there was no one listed by that name. Google searches proved just as futile, which Sadie found both frustrating and surprising. In a city the size of San Francisco, surely there could be at least one Zane Grey, couldn't there?

Switching tactics, she considered her trip to Manning

Property Holdings the day before. Assuming the victim tended to date the same type of men, she might be wise to focus on business enterprises. Over the better part of the next hour, she scouted the rosters of real estate companies, financial institutions, and other similar businesses. She found not even one deviation of the name she was looking for. In fact, she didn't find so much as a single name beginning with the letter *Z*.

Sadie looked over the order form again. As with the others, she did have a phone number she could call. But her reason for not trying that was solid. If one of these three men was a killer, the last thing she wanted was to draw attention to herself. Her number was a local area code too. It was just too risky. But, on the other hand, if she weren't the one to place the call…

Leaving her office, she hurried through the store, passing one customer who was trying on a red beret in front of a mirror and another who was purchasing three of the garden rose lotion bottles. Giving Amber a thumbs-up signal, Sadie scooted out the front door and over to Matteo's shop.

"No," Matteo said once Sadie waited for his line of customers to temporarily dwindle.

"Just one call?" Sadie said.

"I've already called them all to tell them the chocolates couldn't be delivered and to issue them refunds," Matteo said. "There's no reason I would call again. And if we're dealing with someone dangerous, I definitely don't want to."

"I understand," Sadie said. After all, it was the same reason she didn't want to call.

Matteo sighed. "I'm sorry. Have a passion fruit pecan truffle. Maybe that will help." He held out a tray. Sadie readily snatched one up, took a bite, and sighed.

"Delicious."

"Thank you."

"Do you remember anything in particular about the phone calls when you made them?" Sadie asked. "Did anything stand out?" She placed her copies of the orders on the counter so Matteo wouldn't have to flip through the batch of papers on his clipboard. Matteo looked each one over.

"I remember I didn't reach anyone directly," Matteo said.

"What do you mean?"

Matteo picked up the paper with Luke Manning's name on it. "This one, for example. I couldn't get through to the guy's office. I had to leave a message with some receptionist. It sounded like it was a fancy office of some sort." He shrugged his shoulders. "Who knows? Maybe it was just some hot dog stand with a woman on a power trip."

Sadie smiled but held back comments as Matteo moved to another sheet. He set it aside quickly to ring up a half pound of vanilla-nut fudge for a customer. He boxed the order and slipped a red ribbon around the package, then turned back to the paper after the customer left.

"I think this one might have answered the phone, but I couldn't hear anything over the noise in the background."

"What kind of noise?" Sadie asked.

"All kinds of noise," Matteo said. "People chattering, some shouting in the background, a bell ringing, some sort of horn going off in the distance. I hope the guy even understood what I was saying. I just ran the refund through. I figure he'll call if the credit doesn't make sense."

Sadie filed that away for future reference and pointed to the third sheet, the one with Zane Grey's name on it. "What about this one?"

Matteo frowned, then grabbed his clipboard and flipped

to the original sheet. He held it up to Sadie, pointing to the handwritten initials "LM."

"You left a message," Sadie said. She jotted the same note when she returned a call and only reached voice mail. "Anything you remember about the recording?"

"Come to think of it, yes," Matteo said. "It was a crazy recording, with music going in the background."

"What kind of music?" Sadie tapped her fingers on the counter.

"Maybe disco? Rock? I don't know," Matteo said. "It was loud enough to make the voice hard to hear. But I remember now it said something like 'Zany's.' Or maybe it was just 'message, please.' Don't know if that's any help at all. People should have the sense to turn their music off before recording a voice mail message." He turned to greet two women who had just entered the store.

"Thank you, Matteo," Sadie said. "That definitely helps." She grabbed one more truffle from the sample tray and slipped out the door.

EIGHT

The battered building in front of Sadie was not at all what she expected. Weathered shingles hung at odd angles, and the neon sign in the cracked front window was askew. She thought she'd dressed down enough to fit in at the dubious establishment, but her rarely worn basic jeans and navy sweatshirt were at least three levels more formal than the attire of others stepping through the front door. It didn't take much imagination to know that the man nosy Mags had described as skinny, sleazy, and slinky was the one Sadie would find here.

Matteo was a lover of Italian opera, a tribute to his own heritage. Sadie knew from previous discussions with him that he listened to nothing else. Hence he wouldn't have recognized the "Zany Z's" reference on the voice mail he reached as being from a common—and annoying—radio commercial for the offbeat bar in the Tenderloin. But Sadie, who flipped stations as frequently as she changed earrings while accessorizing an outfit, knew it immediately, simply because the ad was so irritating. That was why she reluctantly headed for one of the least reputable areas in the city and now stood before the derelict building, listening to a blast of Metallica flow out the front door each time it opened.

Sadie approached the entrance with a mix of trepidation and curiosity, but not fear. She'd never had trouble standing up for herself, the timidity gene being completely absent from her genetic makeup. So when the ID-checking bouncer stopped her at the door to ask if she needed help, she puffed her chest out and shouted loud enough to be heard above the music. "Do I look like I need help, buddy?" All trace of her usual societal demeanor gone in one Oscar-worthy moment, she passed the obvious entrance exam and walked right in.

Brave as she felt after stepping into her tough-woman mode, she was relieved to have let Amber care for Coco. Zany Z's was no place for a sophisticated Yorkie, not to mention how badly her floral tote bag would have clashed with her outfit. Besides, while a few tattered paper bowls of pretzels dotted the mismatched tables and bar top, the only bones in sight were stenciled on the wall behind grinning skulls. No, this was no place for... well, anyone. Yet Sue Bennett must have made an appearance at some point unless she knew Zane from somewhere else.

Sadie made her way to the bar, doing her best to imitate walks she'd observed in biker movies. A few sideways glances from others told her she might not be pulling it off accurately, but she reached the bar nonetheless and ordered: "what that guy down there is having." She nodded sharply to a man at the end of the bar and prayed she'd be able to chug down whatever it was without choking.

The bartender, a voluptuous woman wearing a tank top so sheer that Sadie wondered why she bothered to wear it at all, plunked a pint of dark brew in front of her and a shot glass of amber liquid beside it. "Twelve bucks for the boilermaker," the woman said. She slapped her hand on the counter, a bizarre mix of rings decking out each finger. The thought crossed Sadie's mind that a punch from that hand could be painful, if not a direct ticket to a dentist's chair.

Fishing some crumpled bills out of her pocket, Sadie

placed the money on the counter, adding in a generous tip. The woman leaned forward, took the money, and winked, a gesture Sadie wasn't even going to attempt to decipher.

While trying to determine if the shot should be tackled before the beer or the beer before the shot, Sadie sat on a bar stool with a slouched posture that seemed appropriate for the ambiance of the place. She looked around, noting a questionable duo in black at a pool table, an exchange of some sort between hands underneath a far corner table, and a group of scantily dressed women hanging out around a man in a booth. The object of the women's effusive attention was tall and skinny, with a grin on his face that could easily be deemed sleazy. There was no question in Sadie's mind that this was Zane himself.

Not wanting to draw the man's attention by staring, Sadie shifted her gaze to the bar's eclectic décor. Vintage photographs of cable cars hung at varying heights on one wall. Most leaned in one direction or the other, and one frame lacked a fourth side. Fishing nets and wire baskets dangled from the ceiling, plastic fish and crabs attached to them in haphazard fashion. Menus from Chinatown restaurants looked up through varnish on a few round bar tables. In every direction, some sort of display detailed aspects of the city by the bay.

Sadie turned back to the bar and eyed the two glasses. She gathered her courage, reached out with one brave swoop of her hand, and downed the shot of whiskey. As she fought back a choking response to the rush of heat through her throat, a man slid onto the bar stool next to her and spoke up.

"Friends in low places, Ms. Kramer?"

Sadie recognized the voice without having to look. *Froggy!*

"Imagine running into you here, Detective," Sadie squeaked,

still recovering from the shock of the whiskey.

"Yes, imagine that," Frogert said. "I was just thinking the same thing. I would have taken you for more of a Palace Hotel tea type of girl."

Sadie grabbed the mug of beer and raised it in the air as if making a toast. "We all need a little variety in our lives, you know." She ventured a sideways glance at the man, wondering if his hairline might have receded a bit more since the day before.

"I can see that." The detective ordered coffee, which soon landed in front of him. He tore open a sugar packet and took his time pouring its contents into the cup. Sadie took a sip of beer and waited for him to speak. She wasn't about to volunteer her reasons for stopping in at Zany Z's. He could do his own investigating. After all, that was his job.

Harsh voices and harsher words accompanied the sound of shattering glass as a fight broke out near the entrance. Sadie turned to see a fist connect with the bouncer's face. In turn, the bouncer strong-armed the source of the punch and shoved him out the front door.

"Way to go, Eddie!" the bartender shouted, twirling a bar towel above her head.

"You tell 'im, Lila!" The cheer came from a burly man with a scruffy beard, which started a chorus of catcalls and whistles.

The man Sadie had pegged as Zane slid out of the booth and stepped behind the bar. He wrapped his arm around Lila's waist, nuzzled his face in her neck, and slapped her derriere before pulling a beer out of a refrigerated compartment behind her and returning to the booth. Lila smiled, though in an odd way, causing Sadie to wonder if the reaction was forced. And had she seen a hint of a wince when Zane first grabbed the woman's waist?

"Just a bit out of your element?" Frogert asked as he took a sip of coffee.

The detective's comment clued Sadie in that her pseudo-biker-chick-tough-woman persona was slipping as she watched the interaction around her. The temporary fun of playing the role had faded quickly in view of broken glass, thrown punches, and a proprietor openly groping an employee. No, she wasn't *just a bit* out of her element. She was way out. And she'd already learned more than she'd expected to; there was no need to linger. She downed the rest of her beer and stood up. "I'm calling it a night. See you soon, Detective."

"Count on it," Frogert said.

NINE

"You went to Zany Z's?" Amber stared at Sadie as if she'd lost her mind.

"Guilty as charged," Sadie said. "First time ever, and I certainly hope the last. Not really my scene. How did you know?"

Amber pointed to Sadie's left arm, which was firmly wrapped around Coco. The Yorkie, though pleased with having Amber as a dog-sitter, had jumped straight into Sadie's arms when she walked in the door.

"Oh right," Sadie said, eyeing the purple Z stamped on her skin. "Personally, I think checking my ID was unnecessary. I should have handed him a Medicare card."

"You don't have a Medicare card," Amber pointed out.

"Minor detail," Sadie said. "I will in a few years. Maybe I should have a fake one made, just for occasions like this. You know, like a fake ID? Eddie would get a kick out of it." Sadie tilted her head to the side as she envisioned the scene. It would almost be worth another trip just to see the bouncer's face when she presented the card.

Amber pulled her jacket on and gave Coco a pat on the head.

"Thanks for watching her and especially for dropping her off," Sadie said.

"You know I don't mind," Amber said. "I'll see you at the shop tomorrow." She smirked on her way out the door, an expression that looked adorable on her smooth, sweet face. "Sleep in if you need to after your wild night."

"Funny." Sadie waved, thanked her again, and then closed the door after Amber left. "Come on, Coco, I need to get out of this crazy getup." Moving to the bedroom, she shed her plain jeans and sweatshirt and donned a pair of hot pink pajamas with a UFO print. Green alien faces peered out of each flying saucer in the pattern. "There," she said. "Much better, don't you think?" Coco stared at her, seemingly unconvinced.

Sadie moved to the kitchen and fixed a cup of tea. Coffee would keep her awake this late, and although she often had half a glass of wine during the evening, she'd had her fill of spirits for the night.

Taking her tea into the living room, she settled into a favorite armchair and ran scenes from the evening through her mind, unsettling as a few of them were. The fight near the bar entrance was a highlight, though she was grateful to not have been sitting nearby. It gave the place an extra spark of authenticity in a surreal way, like being in a movie yet watching it at the same time. Most telling was "Zany" Zane's treatment of the bartender, which was a testament to his true character, or lack thereof. And the more she thought about it, the clearer it seemed that woman's inner reaction didn't match the smiling front she'd put on. Replaying the scene in her head, the wince she'd questioned at first was not imagined.

Turning her thoughts to Sue Bennett, she tried to fathom the connection between the everyday woman she'd observed on the customer's visits to Flair and the low-life bar proprietor. It seemed incongruous to think of her dating someone like Zane. She had always been a quiet customer, choosing clothing purchases that were conservative and somewhat boring.

Almost as difficult to imagine was a relationship to Luke Manning. Someone of his standing in the business world might be more suited for an upscale—dare she say snobby—companion like the woman who entered Manning Property Holdings while she was there—fashionably dressed, with a refined aura about her.

Another possibility hit her, one she could barely believe she hadn't thought of before. Not all chocolate is necessarily ordered by those with romantic intentions. Could any of the men be a brother? A father? *Certainly not Zane!* A business manager? There were many possibilities. But... the train of thought derailed quickly when she fetched the order copies and read small, scribbled notes at the bottom of each sheet. Cards had been included with all the orders. The first was from Luke. "Happy Valentine's Day." Well, that one was pretty generic and certainly not original. It might be from a relative, but most likely it wasn't. The second, from Zane, read "To my one and only." *Ha, that one was hard to believe!*

The third card was puzzling. "My beautiful little crab lady?" Now there was a Valentine greeting you didn't hear every day. Sadie shook her head. No one had ever sent her a note like that, much less attached to custom chocolate truffles in a fancy heart-shaped box. It was peculiar. Why not "My beautiful little kitten?" or "My sweet petunia?" Granted the last sounded a little saccharine-ish. But my little crab lady? Didn't that sound a little... er, crabby?

Unless... A realization flashed through Sadie's mind. An odd message like that usually had a special meaning to the giver and recipient, an inside joke, or just a unique set of interests or circumstances. Taking this approach, there were a few ways she could interpret the card that had accompanied that particular box of chocolates.

"Maybe it was an apology, Coco," Sadie said. "Maybe the victim had been acting crabby, and the gift sender—Bruno, in this case—felt he was to blame, and the card was a teasing way of saying he was sorry." As she explained it to Coco, it already sounded weak. Unless the victim had been the one apologizing for being in a foul mood recently and this was the sender's way of accepting her apology. Still, all in all, that theory was a stretch.

Grabbing her cell phone, she put in a quick call to Amber, knowing she would have just arrived home and would still be awake. Amber answered on the second ring.

"Amber," Sadie said. "I have an odd question for you."

"Shoot," Amber replied.

"Did Sue Bennett ever mention plans when she was purchasing items from you? Like where she might be going that she needed a new outfit, anything like that?" It wasn't really a strange question at all. Customers often said they needed something to wear for an upcoming luncheon or a special occasion or simply because they were tired of what was in their closets. Discussions about the reason for shopping were pretty common while people debated between outfits. And if in a hurry, they were even more likely to say something. For example, "I only have ten minutes and I need something new for a date tonight." That sort of thing.

"Nothing that I can remember," Amber said. "Except..."

"Except what?"

Amber yawned, causing Sadie to feel slightly guilty for not waiting until the morning to ask her to recall Sue Bennett's shopping occasions.

"Now that I think about it, she did make a comment a couple of weeks ago when she picked up a lace camisole. I remember thinking it seemed out of the ordinary for her,"

Amber said. "She was looking for something 'a little sexy.' Those were her own words, and she blushed after describing it that way."

Sadie tried to imagine the quiet woman requesting anything other than conservative clothing. "Did she say why?" *A silly question,* Sadie thought. Customers might describe what they were looking for but rarely got into personal details.

"Only that she was going out to dinner that evening," Amber said. "Oh wait. For seafood. I remember that because I asked if she was going to Alioto's or Scoma's."

Aha! Sadie's mood perked up. That would give her a lead if she knew where the woman planned to dine. Even better if she had an excuse to follow up and treat herself to a meal at one of the city's well-known restaurants. "So, was she?"

"No," Amber said, shooting down Sadie's hopes for a fancy night out. "She said she'd just be eating at one of the little sidewalk shacks along Jefferson Street."

"Huh. It's odd that she'd want something sexy to wear just for that," Sadie said. "Unless she had plans afterward, I suppose."

Amber yawned again. "Maybe. I wasn't about to ask, and she didn't volunteer a reason."

"I'll let you go," Sadie said. "Thanks."

"Not sure if that helped," Amber said, "but happy to oblige."

"Get some rest. I'll see you at the shop tomorrow, figure in the afternoon. I have an errand to run in the morning." Sadie ended the call and mulled over Amber's comments. They might not lead to any new information, but there was one plus to it: Sadie now had an excuse to visit one of her favorite San Francisco haunts.

TEN

With her tote bag securely slung over her shoulder, Sadie hopped the Powell-Hyde cable car line and headed to Fisherman's Wharf. The well-known San Francisco mode of transportation was not only a popular attraction for tourists, it also made for an easy way to avoid crowded parking lots and the near-impossible city street parking. She'd always been grateful that the penthouse she and Morris had shared was in convenient proximity to the cable car route. Now, on her own, she was even more appreciative.

The delectable aroma of freshly baked sourdough bread surrounded Sadie as she walked along Jefferson Street, the hub of wharf activity. Large cauldrons of boiling water prepared local Dungeness crab that passersby could purchase and eat on the go or at wooden countertops along the boardwalk. Stacks of bundled whole crab sat ready for customers to take home or have shipped. Oysters on the half shell, shrimp cocktails, and lobster-filled square paper trays, ready for hungry customers, offered other options for those seeking out the variety of seafood available.

Sadie had never been able to resist grabbing something to eat at Fisherman's Wharf. The sounds, smells, and hustle and bustle of activity simply begged for a dip into the local culture. Ordering a traditional favorite, clam chowder served in a sourdough bread bowl, she stood at a wooden countertop and dipped her spoon into the creamy mixture. She closed her eyes and sighed. Chowder never tasted as good anywhere else, partially because of tradition and atmosphere, but also because it was just plain delicious. Even Coco, not one for seafood, poked her head out of the tote bag to try to steal a bit of the bread.

Pausing for the meal gave Sadie a chance to look around and consider options. All she'd been able to find about Bruno was that he might work at the wharf. He could be one of the multigenerational Italian fishermen whose ancestors first brought the crab fishing to the area. Or he might be a vendor, someone she'd seen in one of the stalls she'd passed. She only had his first name to go on, but at least it was something. Enough questioning might lead her in the right direction—after she finished her clam chowder, of course.

Still, the main puzzle in her mind continued to grow. How was it that the victim was associated with men of such varied backgrounds? And well enough that they all ordered special Valentine chocolate assortments for her. She mulled over possible connections while taking time to enjoy the thick, creamy chowder. Dropping small pieces of bread into her tote bag periodically, she finally finished the meal and reluctantly threw the remainder of the bread bowl away in a trash container.

Sadie glanced around, relieved that Frogert—*Froggy*—was nowhere in sight. Without a doubt, she'd be able to learn more without his shadow looming over her. She was also aware that her persistence in chasing down the three men who had ordered the chocolates might make her look even more suspect than she already did. The thought annoyed her, thinking of Mags taking down the license plate to her car and passing it on to the police. To begin with, she had nothing to do with the murder. Her presence at the scene was clear, and she'd explained it as such. Apparently, Mags was not only a busybody but an untrusting person with an active imagination. As a result, Sadie was stuck in the middle of a murder investigation.

For a good portion of an hour, Sadie went from vendor to vendor, inquiring about the name Bruno. Either no one had heard of him or they weren't willing to admit it, or they knew multiple men named Bruno. She even broke down and bought a whole crab to take home from a couple working at one stand, thinking that chatting with the man cracking the crab for her would open up his willingness to pass on information. Each time the man pounded a crab leg with his mallet, she came up with a different approach. But the more she lingered, the more the woman shot her angry looks, and the man became impatient to move on to the next customer.

In the end, her attempts to find any trace of Bruno were futile, aside from having the cracked crab to look forward to that evening—a plus, needless to say. She picked up a fresh sourdough loaf to accompany the crab later and headed back home.

* * *

Amber looked up from the store counter as Sadie entered. A telltale blush on her cheeks and a small stack of new deliveries told Sadie that Amber's favorite UPS driver had stopped by.

"So?" Sadie asked, hoping for a progress report from her young manager. She wasn't usually one to play matchmaker, but Amber felt like a daughter to her, and Dylan seemed like a good guy. She just wanted them both to be happy.

"So," Amber said, blushing even more, "he asked me out."

"Finally!" Sadie clapped her hands together, her enthusiasm

causing clunky wooden bangles to clatter against each other. "And you didn't even have to hint."

Amber smiled. "Nope. He just asked me out of the blue. It was funny; he was nervous!"

"I'm not surprised." Sadie laughed. "You two have been stalling for ages."

"I suppose we have," Amber admitted.

"So is this for Valentine's Day?" Sadie asked.

"Yes, but lunch, not dinner," Amber said. "So no stress on romance."

Sadie nodded with approval. "A good plan. Smart guy. Still, a little romantic, I think." She started back to her office, only to hear Amber call after her.

"Oh, by the way, speaking of romance…" Amber's voice had a teasing tone to it. "Your *own* boyfriend called. I put the note on your desk."

"Which one?" Sadie quipped, a twinkle in her eye. Without waiting for an answer, she entered the back office and looked at the message. *Ah, not the one I'd prefer to hear from,* she thought, seeing Detective Frogert's name on the paper. Deciding there was nothing to be gained by stalling, she dialed his number.

"I recommend the shrimp cocktail next time," Frogert said. "It's quite good."

Sadie sighed. "You're following me." Was she surprised, or simply annoyed?

"Maybe you're following me," Frogert said.

"Hardly." *Annoyed, definitely annoyed.*

Not wasting any more time on small talk, Frogert continued. "I received a call today from a friend of yours. Apparently, you're well connected with the New Orleans police."

"Broussard called you?" This took Sadie by surprise. It

hadn't occurred to her that he might check into the situation himself. She'd only called him for advice.

"In your best interest, I might add," Frogert said. "He'd make a good character witness for you if you ever get into serious trouble."

"Your statement implies I'm not in serious trouble," Sadie said. "Glad to hear that."

"No. As much as I've enjoyed our *coincidental* meetings, I don't believe you're involved in this," Frogert said. "I've spoken with Margaret Gabston numerous times now, and she's implicated at least twenty people, ranging from you to the Pope. We generally refer to this type of help as unreliable."

Sadie debated whether to ask if Mags AKA Gladys had any other conspiracy theories or simply to compliment Froggy on his sarcastic sense of humor—something she highly admired in people—but decided to remain quiet.

"So I believe we can now stop running into each other," Frogert said.

Sadie nodded, knowing the translation of this sentence was "back off." *Maybe I will, maybe I won't,* Sadie mused. She'd never been one to easily shrug off curiosity.

"Are we in agreement on this?" Frogert asked.

"Of course," Sadie said. After all, she was all for the idea of not running into Froggy again. Naturally, she was going to agree. After a few polite parting comments, the call ended.

Sadie returned to the front of the store to see if Amber needed anything.

"Any news?" Amber asked.

"Just that I'm not a hardened criminal, apparently," Sadie said. She gave Coco a pat on the head, which the Yorkie gladly received.

Amber added more bottles of hand lotion to the counter

display, restocking some she had sold earlier. "Well, I'm glad to hear that."

Sadie picked up Coco, got her situated in the tote bag, and then headed out. She had a phone call to make and planned to make it from home.

ELEVEN

"You called Froggy?"

Sadie had barely taken the time to pour herself a glass of chardonnay—much more appealing than that boilermaker she'd managed to force down at Zany Z's—before picking up her phone and calling Broussard. She was flattered that he had taken the time to call in a positive word for her with the SFPD. But it wasn't something he needed to do, and she worried it might backfire if Detective Frogert felt she had a law enforcement friend interfering.

"Ms. Kramer," Broussard said when he picked up the phone.

"Detective Broussard," Sadie replied, in keeping with their traditionally formal greetings.

"Yes," Broussard said. "I did call Detective Frogert. I admit that I was concerned with having your license plate associated with the crime scene. I apologize if you felt I was interfering. But it's also not uncommon for departments to compare cases and details. It did sound like a curious set of circumstances."

"Did you find out any more details?" Sadie asked. She took a sip of wine and paced her living room. "There hasn't been much else in the paper since the first article. Only that they suspected foul play."

"There probably won't be more details right away," Broussard said. "A lot of that is kept under wraps during an open investigation. Letting the information out can make it tougher to find the guilty party. The less that person knows that we know, the more chance we have of catching him. Or her. I don't mean to not sound like an equal opportunity accuser."

"An admirable trait," Sadie said, sitting down. Her relaxation was short-lived, however, as Broussard spoke up again quickly.

"I did find out some interesting details that I can divulge though." His voice trailed off as if to tease Sadie.

"Really?" Sadie jumped out of her chair eagerly. The sudden movement caused a splash of wine to slip over the edge of her glass, which she ignored. "What did you find out?"

"The most interesting thing, totally unexpected," Broussard said.

Even more eager now, Sadie ran the possibilities through her head. Cause of death? Murder weapon? Suspects narrowed down? She could hardly wait to find out.

Broussard coughed and then cleared his throat. "There's a bar out there in your city that might be connected to the case. It's owned by one of the men who ordered the chocolate."

Yes! Sadie thought. This was exactly what she hoped to hear.

"And this bar had the most unexpected visitor last night. I believe the exact description was 'a senior citizen doing a poor imitation of a biker walk.'"

No! This was definitely not what she wanted to hear. But there was no getting out of it now. She sat back down and surrendered. She knew where the conversation was headed.

"Aside from the fact the bar doesn't sound like a smart place to hang out, I worry about you getting near those guys who sent the chocolates. They're obvious suspects, even though they could all be innocent. Keeping your distance is the smart thing to do. You really don't have anything to do with this, Sadie."

"That's not entirely correct," Sadie protested. "I was at the scene of the crime, heading for the victim's house, and was carrying deliveries from three different suspects. Plus that nosy Mags person reported my vehicle's license plate. It seems I was involved from the start, whether I wanted to be or not."

"All true," Broussard said. "For someone not involved, you managed to be in the wrong place at the wrong time, with potential evidence in your hands."

"Well, you see?" Sadie countered. "Now that you put it that way, I rest my case."

"Fine," Broussard said. "But how about not playing amateur sleuth on this one anymore? I'd certainly feel more comfortable knowing you were staying out of danger. And I'm sure the SFPD will do their job with or without your help, possibly more easily without it."

Sadie considered arguing the last point but thought better of it.

"Do we have a deal?" Broussard waited patiently for an answer.

"I think we do," Sadie said, not even bothering to cross her fingers this time. He had a good point, that the police would do their job with or without her. And it was touching that he was personally concerned for her safety. Maybe she would just stay out of it and let Froggy hop around doing the work. At that thought, she burst out laughing.

"Sadie?"

"I'm sorry," Sadie said, still laughing. "Just a funny image that popped into my mind. It's nothing important."

Broussard's voice softened. "How about I check in with you tomorrow just so I know you're staying out of trouble?"

"I wouldn't mind that at all," Sadie said. That strange fluttering feeling hit her that she felt sometimes when talking to Broussard. "I'll most likely be at the shop. It should be a busy day with last-minute Valentine sales. I'll either be there or I'll be at home, one or the other."

"That's a comforting thought," Broussard said. "Stick to your shop and home until this blows over. I don't need to remind you that an arrest hasn't been made yet, do I? There's a killer out there somewhere."

"On that pleasant note…" Sadie sighed.

"I'm just trying to keep you out of trouble."

"I appreciate that," Sadie said, realizing this was true. It felt good to know he cared about her safety even if it would mean keeping her curiosity in check.

With a few more words of goodbye, the call ended. Sadie looked around for Coco and patted her lap. Coco immediately jumped up. "Looks like we have to cool it with the snooping around."

Coco looked at her with a dubious expression.

Sadie had to admit: wise as the plan was, even she wondered if she could pull it off.

TWELVE

As Sadie expected, Flair was busy the next day. In fact, it was more than busy; it matched the frenzy of opening day at AT&T Park. There was always something different about the approach of Valentine's Day too. Whereas the shop usually saw almost entirely female customers, this was a time when Sadie and Amber could count on men to arrive instead of the boutique's usual women customers who tended to browse and enjoy the shopping experience itself. Men had a different energy about them at this time, which could easily be summed up in one word: panic.

Sadie had anticipated the unique challenge after years of handling Valentine's Day, Christmas, birthdays, and anniversaries, which were similar in last-minute activity. The men who stopped in needed a gift, they needed it now, and they had no idea what to get. That created a challenge for Sadie and Amber, but they were prepared for it, even enjoyed it.

"You were smart to order in those simple heart necklaces this year." Amber complimented Sadie as she sipped on what Sadie expected was her usual double espresso from Jay's Java Joint.

"Thanks," Sadie said, eyeing the sterling silver chains with a dangling heart, presented in a box small enough to be elegant but not so small as to mislead the recipient about its contents. Each heart featured a tiny diamond just off-center.

This made the piece a sweet choice for those who weren't able or willing to pick up something pricier at the local jeweler.

"These should help with the indecisive customers too." Sadie moved to a shelf of cashmere scarves in a rainbow of colors. With wind and fog common to San Francisco, a soft scarf was always a good accessory to have on hand, no matter what season. It also served as a sweet but nonromantic option for those choosing a gift for a mother, sister, or secretary. Valentine's gifts were not always intended just for sweethearts.

Sadie adjusted the angle of one of Matteo's specialty heart-shaped gift boxes, which was displayed on a miniature easel. "Cioccolato will be swamped today, but we'll still want to suggest customers stop by there to add something sweet to whatever they choose here."

Amber laughed. "This would have nothing to do with the fact that Matteo said we could eat the contents of the display box if we did, would it?"

"That's a bonus, I admit," Sadie said. "But we always want to send him business, just like he sends people over to us."

"You two are great next-door business neighbors," Amber said. She stepped up to the register to ring up a soft pink sweater, a gift for an elderly mother.

"Wonderful choice, Andrew," Sadie said, recognizing the regular customer. "How is your mother doing?"

"Still bedridden," the man said. "But she loves wearing something special around her shoulders. It cheers her up." He put his credit card in his wallet after Amber handed it back to him. "I have a stack of sweet romance novels to go with it," he said.

Sadie nodded with approval. "An excellent combination." She thanked the customer and crossed the room to help a tall man with a puzzled expression. He frowned as he held an item in each hand, debating between a red silk blouse and a fluffy chenille bathrobe.

"Does the person you're buying the gift for like to go out to social events?" Sadie asked. "Or does she prefer to spend time at home, reading or watching television shows and movies?"

"It's for my wife," the man said. "We go out on occasion, but given a choice, she prefers to stay in. We watch a lot of classic movies."

"I vote for the bathrobe, in that case," Sadie said. "Nothing beats curling up on a couch and being comfortable at home. She can always return it if she prefers something else." Sadie took the bathrobe to the front counter, removed the price tag, and wrapped the item in white tissue paper. She placed it in a glossy red handle bag and tied the handles with white ribbons that cascaded over the edges. Amber rang up the sale, and the man left, content with his purchase. As he exited the shop, a woman entered, catching Sadie's attention.

"What is it?" Amber said, noticing an odd look on Sadie's face.

"I know that woman, the one with the sunglasses on." Sadie kept her voice soft. "At least I think I do." She fought to place the connection as she watched the customer wander from rack to rack. The woman seemed only semifocused on the selections as she looked around. Unable to see her eyes, Sadie tried to judge the direction of the woman's gaze by the tilt of her head.

"I don't recognize her, but I love that scarf she's wearing," Amber whispered. "It looks expensive. I bet she's not going to buy anything. She's got that browsing mode about her."

Sadie nodded. "You're right. She's just looking around. But she doesn't seem like the shoplifting type either." Flair rarely had a problem with merchandise disappearing, but occasionally something would show up missing. It was just an unfortunate part of retail.

A line formed at the sales counter, causing the discussion to pause. Amber rang up a silk blouse, cultured pearl earrings, and a red wallet with fringe trim, passing them to Sadie for bags, tissue, and ribbon. Midway through the flurry of activity, the woman who had been browsing left the store.

"I think she might have gone to Matteo's shop," Amber said, once there was a break in the line. "At least I saw her turn in that direction."

"Do me a favor," Sadie said, an uncomfortable hunch forming. "Run over there and check. I'll cover the register. Don't say anything to her. Just see if she's there."

Amber looked at Sadie, eyebrows raised. "You're passing up an opportunity to go to Matteo's yourself? With that sample tray he keeps out?"

"Just this one time," Sadie said. "I won't make a habit of it, I assure you." She turned toward an approaching customer as Amber ran next door.

"Which do you think?" A man held up two necklaces, one a trendy strand of beads, the other a simple amethyst pendant.

"What colors does she usually wear?" Sadie asked.

The customer thought over the question. "Orange, yellow, red, usually something bright."

"I'd go with the strand of beads," Sadie suggested. "It will match more of her clothing." Placing the necklace in a small gift box, she thanked the man for his purchase.

Amber returned as the man walked out. "No sign of her." Amber shrugged her shoulders. "But is it ever crowded over there!"

"I'm sure it is," Sadie said. "This is Matteo's busiest day of the year. Thanks for checking," she added. "I'll be in the office if you need me. Just buzz the intercom, and I'll come rescue you."

Settled in the office, Sadie contemplated the strange behavior of the woman. Although she hadn't been able to see her face clearly, she was almost positive it was the stylish woman she'd seen at Luke Manning's office. The real question was: Had the woman stopped by to see the store? Or had she come by to check up on Sadie? And, if so, why?

THIRTEEN

Still mulling over the odd visit in the shop the day before, Sadie set the visit aside to pursue a different aspect of the puzzle. She'd found two of the three men who'd sent chocolate to the victim, but not the third.

"What do you say we go try to find this Bruno character, Coco?" She didn't have to beg. Coco always responded with enthusiasm to "go." Hearing one of her favorite words, she immediately trotted over to Sadie's tote bag and hopped in.

The fog outside looked heavier than usual and the sky above it darker. It provided a welcome opportunity to wear one of the fashionable new rain ponchos that the shop had started carrying. The bright umbrella print was cheerful and somehow made the poncho feel more functional, as far as Sadie was concerned. California wasn't prone to rain, but it never hurt to be prepared. After all, it was February, and spring was on its way—April showers and all that. Rain could always arrive early.

Sadie slid her arm through the handles of her tote bag, letting it dangle from the crook of her elbow, and headed back to Fisherman's Wharf.

The cable car's brakes squealed as it pulled to a stop a few blocks from the wharf. Sadie stepped off and headed for Jefferson Street. The mixed smells of salt water, seafood, and baking bread beckoned to her as she approached. Her stomach rumbled at the thought of another sourdough bread bowl filled with clam chowder. Or maybe she should have a shrimp cocktail, as Froggy had suggested. Or a crab salad. Or some oysters on the half shell with enough horseradish and cocktail sauce to disguise the fact they were rather slimy. Or, heck—why not some of each?

Pushing the thought of food out of her mind, she turned her focus to the purpose of her trip: she was determined to find Bruno this time. No matter how many bread bowls of chowder it took. Maybe she'd even need to make a side trip to Ghirardelli Square. *No harm in a few perks along the way.*

As usual, Fisherman's Wharf was busy. Tourists crowded the area, wandering along Pier 39 to visit shops and hovering over the sea lion colony, eager to get a few photos to show off when they returned home. Some visited other attractions, touring the USS *Pampanito*, a World War II submarine, or playing vintage games in the Musée Mécanique. Occasionally Sadie enjoyed taking in different San Francisco landmarks, even though she lived right there in the city. She knew from traveling that people often visited spots far away from home yet not the ones in their own backyards. But today she was on a mission and headed straight for the seafood stands.

Grabbing a paper cup of crab and cocktail sauce, she consumed the delicacy as slowly as possible, using the time to look around. A similar hustle and bustle hummed along the stretch, with now familiar-looking faces manning the stands. Vendors called out to each other, often with names, which Sadie found helpful. But Joe, Rudy, Steve, and Tony weren't the names she was hoping to hear.

She continued on, passing the booth where the man had been cracking crab with a mallet on her first visit. He worked alone this time, without the woman partner who had given her the evil eye before. She considered stopping to chat with him but thought better of it. She'd lingered at that stand before and less at others that she could further explore this time. As she passed by the booth, however, a comment from a vendor at the next stand caused her to pause.

"Working alone today, Brownie? Did Gina leave you on your own?"

It was an innocent comment from a neighboring vendor who was arranging oysters on a tub of ice in his display window. But it represented more to Sadie, whose high school Italian brought back a random fact. "Bruno" was Italian for "brown," hence the nickname Brownie could be… couldn't it?

"Nah, she's just out and about," the crab-cracking man called back.

"What do you think, Coco?" she whispered to her tote bag. Coco stuck her head out, looked at the oysters with disdain, and retreated back inside. "You're no help at all," Sadie teased, though with compassion. Oysters weren't among her favorite foods either.

Without an easy way to linger undetected, she moved on, knowing she could return later for additional espionage. She made her way several stands down and picked up a small shrimp salad, another excuse to pause. This time a small table was available against an inner wall, barely large enough to be able to sit, and she had to balance her tote on her lap. Still, it was convenient as a place to ponder the comments she'd overheard.

Sadie squeezed fresh lemon on her salad, looking casually back in the direction of Brownie's booth, as well as taking stock of other customers. She eyed a sourdough bread bowl of chowder passing by and smiled at a young boy pretending to fish from each stand with an invisible fishing pole. A tourist sauntered by with a sizable bag from Ghirardelli Square. This almost erased Sadie's train of thought, but not quite. She still suspected "Brownie" could well be the "Bruno" she was looking for.

Coco let out a sharper-than-usual yip, and Sadie looked down at her with surprise. It wasn't unusual for Coco to comment, but this tiny bark seemed more intense than usual. Sadie hushed her gently, expecting the Yorkie to retreat into the bag. But another yip followed. Curious, Sadie followed Coco's gaze, which aimed in the opposite direction of the stand she'd been intent on observing. There, several small tables away, sat the woman from Brownie's stand, the one who had glared at her on the first trip. Sadie took stock of the woman's companion and drew her breath in, a quick-thinking alternative to a verbal exclamation that might have attracted attention. Across from Gina sat the bartender from Zany Z's. Sadie recalled another customer there calling her Lila.

Sadie lowered her eyes quickly and pulled the hood of her poncho up over her head, grateful the rainwear could double as a disguise. Although she'd only seen each woman once before, the chance of being recognized by either one was too risky.

In addition to the distance between Sadie's table and that of the two women, the conversation was out of hearing range other than a few random phrases when one or the other raised her voice and then had it shushed back down. Sadie was certain she heard "not worth it" tossed out during a pre-shush exclamation, as well as "a bad plan."

Tugging the hood forward to help hide her face, she looked down into her bag, pretending to rummage. Coco, who had a habit of treating this as a game, scurried back and forth inside the bag, play-biting Sadie's fingers.

"Not now, Coco," Sadie whispered. "We can play later. Right now I'm trying to listen." Not only that, but she was trying to figure out why Gina and Lila would even be together. Why would these two women know each other? It couldn't be a coincidence, could it? Two girlfriends or wives of men who were cheating on them with the victim? The plot was definitely thickening. Now if only…

The far-fetched thought had barely crossed Sadie's mind when she glanced up and saw another figure approaching. The woman's nonchalant movements were so much so as to not seem nonchalant in the least. Dressed in similar refined fashion to that which Sadie had seen her wearing in Luke Manning's office, Sadie was now certain this was the woman who had been browsing at Flair. She even sported the same scarf Amber had admired. The woman looked like—there was simply no point in avoiding the cliché, given the perfect setting—a fish out of water.

With her stilettos clicking against the walkway, the woman paused at a busy stand and lifted a sheet of paper off a stack of order forms. She scribbled ten seconds worth of writing but didn't hand it to the vendor. Rather, she folded the paper in half and then in half again, her perfectly manicured nails and shimmering rock on her ring finger making the action look dramatic, as if straight out of a Hitchcock movie. Moving on, she sauntered by the table where Gina and Lila sat. But instead of sitting with them, as Sadie expected, she simply slipped the folded paper onto the table and continued on.

Well, Sadie thought. *Let's just see what happens next.*

From Sadie's vantage point, it wasn't clear who opened the note. Only that—based on four elbows shifting positions—both Gina and Lila were reading the message. A minute later, both women stood and followed the third.

Sadie waited a few moments, just enough to not seem obvious yet not enough to lose track of the trio. Keeping her poncho's hood pulled forward, she maneuvered the crowded walkway as best she could considering the loss of peripheral vision the garment caused. She rounded the end of the block and observed the three women gathered by a railing alongside a pier.

With the women away from the main crowd of people, there was no way Sadie could approach without making herself known, so she had to settle for watching from afar. Unable to overhear anything, the overall picture was still clear: whatever the discussion involved, it wasn't pleasant. Arms flew with gestures of frustration, feet stomped more than once, and even one stilettoed foot tapped impatiently. Voices, though muffled, rose and fell. The subject matter was heated, and three participants were not at all in agreement.

As quickly as the trio's meetup had started, it was over. Sadie watched as Gina headed back to the crab stand. The other two women took off in different directions, neither one bothering to glance back.

"Curiouser and curiouser, Coco," Sadie muttered under her breath. She'd always been fond of the Lewis Carroll phrase from *Alice in Wonderland*. It applied to so many situations that she seemed to find herself in.

Not risking another trip along the vendor stands for fear of attracting Gina's attention, she left Fisherman's Wharf and caught the next cable car home.

FOURTEEN

"What? Are you and Froggy best friends now?" Sadie sighed. She had to admit she was charmed by the upswing of phone calls from Broussard. It had been years since a man had caught her attention in a—dare she say it—romantic sense. Still, it was cramping her amateur-detective style to have not one but two detectives to deal with. It was so much easier to snoop around without actual law enforcement getting in the way.

"I spoke to him because I turned up a few bits of information on my own," Broussard said, "aside from simply looking out for you since you seem determined to stay involved."

Sadie could tell Broussard was smiling, just by the tone of his voice. "I appreciate your concern." This was true. It felt good to know he cared. "And… is there a chance you might want to share these bits of information that you found? Or is that against the rules?" This time she knew the detective was smiling, without even having to hear him speak.

"As I'm sure you know, I can't divulge specific information, but there are a few general comments I can make."

"I'm all ears," Sadie said. She walked to her kitchen, one arm holding the phone to her ear, the other reaching for a wineglass. She'd already changed into a fluffy chenille bathrobe and bunny slippers after arriving home an hour earlier. The trip to the wharf, followed by checking in to see how Amber was faring at the boutique, followed by a quick bite of take-out Chinese that she'd picked up after closing the store, all added up to a full day. She was ready to relax. She poured a half glass of cabernet sauvignon and retired to the living room couch as Broussard filled her in as much as he could.

"You're saying that Manning Property Holdings has a shady real estate deal going on? And that Sue Bennett was somehow involved with it?" Sadie's mind flipped quickly to another real estate deal she'd watched turn into a mess recently.

"No," Broussard said. "I'm not saying that. I don't believe I mentioned any names, for one thing. I'm not sure this case has anything to do with real estate or even with that company. I just know there's a possibility."

"In what way?" Sadie asked.

"I can't say any more. And that's really all I know," Broussard said. "It may have no bearing on this crime at all."

"Real estate certainly seems to be a hot topic these days," Sadie commented.

"Real estate involves money," Broussard said. "And where there's money, there's room for disagreement, which can lead to heated emotions, which can lead to problems. It's just something we always look into."

"Hence the expression 'follow the money,'" Sadie said. She took a sip of wine, thinking that over. Most of the conflicts she'd seen did seem to revolve around finances in some way.

"Yes," Broussard said. "Money is a powerful motive for a lot of things, crime included."

"So is emotion," Sadie pointed out. "And I think emotion may have more to do with this case than money."

Silence on the line. This was not a good thing, Sadie thought. Either Broussard disagreed or she'd just let on that she'd done more snooping than he already thought.

"How about explaining that," Broussard said.

Sadie pulled her thoughts together quickly. "Sue Bennett had chocolate sent to her by three different men, which implies emotional involvement of some sort."

"Possibly," Broussard said. "People could have many reasons for sending chocolate."

"This was *not* just ordinary chocolate!" Sadie exclaimed. "These were satin boxes of Matteo's famous Valentine truffle assortments!" *Really,* Sadie thought to herself, *there is chocolate, and then there is* chocolate! She was not about to let Matteo's exquisite creations be referred to at a common level.

Broussard spoke cautiously. "I will remember to keep chocolate on my list of sensitive topics from now on."

"Good," Sadie said, considering this a consciousness-awakening moment for Broussard.

"I don't suppose I can convince you to back off from this," Broussard said.

"I'll consider it if you can get Froggy to stop pestering me," Sadie said. "Or those women. If I see another one of them in my shop, I'll start thinking I'm being set up."

More silence on the line. *Oops!*

"What women?"

Sadie knew that was coming as soon as the words slipped out. "I think it's more complicated than just the three men who ordered the *chocolate.*" She made sure to emphasize the word "chocolate" to additionally clarify Matteo's quality. "It seems there's a woman behind each man in question."

"Why does that not surprise me?" Broussard's tone told Sadie he was grinning.

"I'm not entirely sure that's funny," Sadie pointed out. "A woman has been murdered after all. At least..." Sadie paused, angling for more information. "This *was* definitely murder, wasn't it? That's not inside information. The newspapers here even refer to it that way."

"Correct," Broussard said. "Murder it is, but let's not get off track here. You were talking about women involved with each of the three men. Why do you think that?"

Sadie knew when she was busted. Besides, she could use his help figuring out the connection. "I saw them together at Fisherman's Wharf today."

"You just happened to be at the wharf again?"

"Let's skip that part for right now," Sadie said. "And for the record, I didn't connect any of this until today. So I wasn't holding back information."

"Fair enough," Broussard said. A pop-top clicked open on the other end of the line, making Sadie momentarily question if a cold soda might taste better than the wine she held.

"I went back to the wharf today," Sadie said, "because it bothered me that I hadn't found the man named Bruno. But I did figure out who he was."

"Not to brag," Broussard said, "but we're ahead of you on that."

"Fine," Sadie said. "Good to see our tax dollars at work. But what about his wife?"

"He's not married, Sadie," Broussard said. "Perhaps detective work isn't the best hobby for you. How about knitting? Cooking? Online poker?"

"Maybe online poker," Sadie said, just to get back at him for giving her a hard time. "But the woman Bruno works with is involved somehow."

"Why do you think that?" Broussard asked, sounding hesitant.

"Because she met up with the other two women," Sadie said. "The bartender from Zany Z's and the fancy woman I saw at Manning Property Holdings."

Broussard was silent. Sadie knew now that she'd hit on something the police hadn't already figured out. Maybe she wouldn't be taking up online poker after all.

"Did they see you?" Broussard finally said.

"No, I'm sure they didn't." Realizing Broussard would now be even more worried, Sadie played it down. "I was several tables away, plus I had my rain poncho on with the hood up. And they were too busy arguing with each other to pay attention anyway."

"Odd," was all Broussard said.

"I thought so too," Sadie said, feeling quite pleased with herself for being on what felt like equal footing with law enforcement.

"All the more reason to stay away," Broussard said.

"Agreed," Sadie said, this time sincerely. At three to one, the odds weren't in her favor. Not to mention Sue Bennett's demise, quite a bad sign in itself.

"By the way, which is your favorite?"

"My favorite?" Sadie repeated. "As in which woman is my hunch for the guilty one?"

Broussard laughed. "No. Your favorite chocolate. The ones your next-door neighbor makes that you claim are so unique."

"His name is Matteo," Sadie clarified. "And it's impossible to choose a favorite. Plus he changes flavors all the time. I'd say the maple-pecan truffle is up there at the top of the list. Also the mango coconut, the cherry-vanilla almond, the cappuccino mint, and the hazelnut caramel. Now that I think about it," Sadie continued, "the pistachio sea salt is also delicious, as is the key lime, which is very delicate…"

"I think I get the picture," Broussard said. "And you get the picture about keeping your distance from those women, right?"

"Yes," Sadie said.

"I know you're going to be curious, so I'll keep you informed on anything I'm allowed to share that Fro—" Broussard coughed and cleared his throat. "That Detective Frogert and I discuss."

Sadie chuckled.

"What?" Broussard asked.

"You almost said 'Froggy.'"

"Good night, Ms. Kramer."

"Good night, Detective Broussard."

FIFTEEN

Sadie thanked a tall, good-looking gentleman for his purchase as she handed him a large bag with two elegant boxes inside. She and Amber had done a fabulous job gift wrapping the identical red silk negligees, not even batting an eye at the possible reasons for the matching items. After all, it wasn't their place to judge. Besides, a sale was a sale. And even Sadie had to admit she'd purchased duplicates of certain clothing that she'd especially loved. Going back to shop for a particular item months later, after deciding it was a favorite, was rarely successful.

The day had started well, with multiple sales within the first hour of business. An elderly woman had purchased whimsical charm bracelets to surprise her granddaughters at a Valentine's brunch. A man with a slight limp had—with much indecision and help—settled on a chenille sweater for his mother. Amber's display of the garden rose hand lotion had solved gift-giving quandaries for several other customers who were looking for something small but thoughtful. It was going to be a good day for business, which was always a good thing.

Taking advantage of a short break in activity, Sadie escaped into her office to take care of miscellaneous business matters. Not nearly as fun as selecting and ordering new items for the shop, bills still needed to be paid, which required matching packing slips with invoices. There were always a few phone calls to answer since busy days tended to send incoming calls to voice mail. Sadie faced a perpetual challenge to keep her desk from becoming an overflowing mound of tasks. The fact she couldn't resist sleuthing challenges on the side didn't help.

Amber stuck her head in the back office. "There's a line at the counter again. Might be good to have backup. Oh, and there's also a customer who seems iffy to me."

"Really? In what way?" Sadie set her paperwork aside and followed Amber back to the front counter, glancing around as she made her way through the shop. Sure enough, an oddly dressed woman stood near a circular rack, her back to the sales counter. One by one, she pulled selections out, either draping them over her arm or replacing them in what Sadie suspected was not the same location on the rounder.

The last behavior in itself wasn't strange. Customers often pulled hangers out, looked selections over, and put them back in haphazard fashion. It was the reason many stores had "go back" racks outside dressing rooms. Flair was a small boutique, so Amber just straightened things up at the end of each day, moving misplaced clothing and accessories to their correct locations. There were far fewer items to rearrange than a department store would have to put away.

Nothing about the customer looked familiar to Sadie, at least not from the back. Her attire was more casual than most of Flair's clientele but several steps above that of a street person and a bit more risqué. The woman's denim miniskirt seemed a little summery for a chilly San Francisco day, and the tie-dyed T-shirt was '60s-style but not currently fashionable. Cowboy boots struck Sadie as an odd footwear choice too, considering the T-shirt. But who was she to judge? Part of the joy of the fashion world was finding one's own individual style. And this was certainly individual.

"Uh-oh," Amber whispered. She nodded her head toward the woman, who was on her way to the dressing room with a good dozen hangers of apparel draped over one arm.

"Uh-oh is right," Sadie said, looking up.

"Exactly," Amber said. "Maybe we should have one of those "six items only" signs on the wall. At least we'd have some control over what customers took back there."

Sadie shook her head. "That's not what I'm worried about. I know who that is." It had only taken a brief glance at the woman's profile once she turned away from the clothing rack to identify her. "That's the bartender from the other night. Her name's Lila."

"From your wild night on the town?" Amber smiled as if in on a well-guarded secret. She paused the discussion to ring up a silver cuff bracelet for a thirty-something gentleman. Setting the jewelry in a gift box that Sadie pulled from under the counter, she added a red ribbon, placed it in a store logo bag, and thanked the customer for his purchase.

"It was hardly a wild night," Sadie said after the man walked away. "I had a drink and took in a little local culture."

Amber laughed. "And watched a bar fight break out."

"Well, yes," Sadie admitted. "There was that." She kept her eyes trained on the dressing room door, wondering if Lila would bring anything to the counter to purchase or if she was there simply to spy on her. Or was she simply getting paranoid?

As if on cue, the dressing room door opened, and Lila emerged with a lacy button-down blouse. As she brought it to the counter, Sadie already wondered how many buttons would remain undone when she wore it.

"Shall I ring this up for you now?" Amber said, adopting a professional tone.

"Yes, please." Lila fished her wallet out of an overstuffed Coach bag. *Knockoff, I bet,* Sadie thought before chastising herself for being catty.

"You look familiar," Lila said, eyeing Sadie. "Do I know you?"

Up close, the woman looked prettier than Sadie remembered, and Sadie took note of the differences. She wore less makeup and had a calmer demeanor. Perhaps the Lila persona she saw at the bar was more of an act than a true personality. It made sense, considering the setting. Tips could be better if she played up to the customers.

"I don't think so," Sadie said calmly. "Maybe you've shopped here before?"

"Never. First time." Lila handed a credit card to Amber. "But you have cute stuff." She picked up a bottle of hand lotion, sniffed it, and set it back down.

"She just has one of those faces," Amber said, redirecting the conversation to a credit card slip for Lila to sign. "You know: the kind everyone recognizes."

"I guess so." Lila shrugged, signed the slip, and put her credit card in her wallet. Amber held the bagged blouse while Lila fought to stuff the wallet back into her purse. A tube of lipstick, roll of breath mints, several crunched-up grocery coupons, and a partially eaten cookie fell out on the counter. Lila picked everything up and stuffed it back into the purse. She zipped it closed with some effort. "Thanks," she said, taking the Flair bag from Amber.

"Knockoff," Amber said as soon as Lila was out the door, causing Sadie to laugh. "What?" She eyed Sadie.

"Nothing." Sadie smiled.

"You know I'm right," Amber whispered as another customer approached the register, this time a man in his forties.

"I'd like to purchase this for my wife," the man said. He brushed the countertop off with one hand before setting a royal blue cardigan sweater down. "This is her favorite color."

"Then I'm glad we had it," Sadie said. She watched as the man straightened the lotion bottle that Lila had left askew. "We don't often have that color. It must have been meant to be."

"Indeed," the man said just before dropping out of sight suddenly. Sadie and Amber exchanged looks. Just as quickly he stood back up, reminding Sadie of a jack-in-the-box toy. "Here," the man said as he placed a small stack of miscellaneous papers on the counter, bundled together with a rubber band. "These were on the floor." He took a handkerchief from his pocket, wiped his hands with it, and put it back in his pocket. "Perhaps a customer dropped them."

"Probably. Thank you for noticing." Sadie picked the papers up quickly, if only to keep the man from being further disturbed by the lack of order he was encountering. "I should put these in the office. Someone may come back for them."

"Good idea," Amber said. "I'm fine now." She waved Sadie away in mock dismissal while asking the customer if he'd like a box and ribbon for the gift.

Sadie carried the small clump of papers to her office. Any one of the day's customers might have dropped them: the woman who purchased the charm bracelet, the limping gentleman who bought the chenille sweater for his mother, or the more recent customer, Lila. This last possibility would be the most opportune, as it might lead to some sort of clue in the Sue Bennett case.

Taking a seat behind her desk, she removed the rubber band and spread the contents out. She often accumulated a similar batch of papers in her own purse: receipts, notes and business cards, nothing out of the ordinary. Every now and then she'd sort through them and throw most of them out, wondering why she'd ever kept them in the first place.

Separating the random papers into categories, she took a closer look at each. There were no credit cards or any type of store card with a name on it. This was smart of the person who'd dropped it but not helpful for anyone wanting to return the papers to their owner. A grocery list, scribbled on a Post-it, was boring at best. A business card from a nail salon had a name scrawled across the top in blue ink but not one she recognized—most likely the manicurist. A second business card from a psychic caused Sadie to lift an eyebrow before setting it aside as silly. Unless, she mused, the psychic had told the person to shop at Flair. Then it wasn't silly at all. She patted the business card in possible appreciation.

Sadie pushed a few more business cards aside and moved on to peruse the coupons. She frowned at a "Buy two cake mixes, get the third free" deal. She never considered that type of promotion real savings. Often the price of the item was raised enough that the three combined totaled the same amount as two on sale would have been. Not to mention the additional calories in this case! The next coupon was tempting—one dollar off a box of Coco's favorite treats. Still, swiping a coupon from someone else without permission would technically be stealing. It was worth one dollar to keep her conscience clear.

Setting the coupons aside, she investigated a handful of folded receipts. Most were for mundane purchases at everyday locations: a gas station, a fast-food burger joint, and groceries. But a fourth one got her attention. Not because the items purchased were of interest—buffalo wings and a soda—but because of the location. *Zany Z's*. An employee discount applied to the total confirmed what she'd originally hoped. Lila, in stuffing spilled items back into her purse, had neglected to notice the bundled papers had fallen on the floor.

Sadie smiled, feeling a sense of accomplishment. Now she was getting somewhere. Or… was she? Her smile faded. So what if Lila liked fast-food burgers and chicken wings? Or had a favorite manicurist? Or sought advice from a psychic? How would any of that link her to Sue Bennett's murder? Unless…

Grabbing the business cards again, Sadie looked at each one. Could there be something that indicated where the three women might have met? The nail salon was a possibility. The psychic? Unlikely. Those sessions would be one-on-one, not a joint activity where the women might meet. A few other cards were also less than fruitful. The automobile club? No, that was not exactly a hub of social activity. A law firm? Interesting, but probably not. The next card, however, caught her interest. *A food bank.*

Sadie leaned back in her chair and pondered the card, waving it in the air as if divining its meaning Johnny Carson style. San Francisco had more than its share of homeless people and an equally proportionate number of food banks that depended on donations from both private citizens and restaurants. That could explain both Zany Z's and Bruno AKA Brownie's crab shack. As for the third woman, perhaps a hoity-toity type might volunteer in order to contribute to society or donate money.

Looking at the back of the card, she noted an inked notation. VBfst2/14. That was clear as… A Canadian zip code came to mind; those always confused her. But on second thought, the scribbled note *was* clear. The food bank would be holding a Valentine's Day breakfast. And, come to think of it, it had been quite a while since she'd volunteered for anything.

SIXTEEN

"Let me get this straight," Matteo said as he prepared to open Cioccolato for the day. "You want me to donate a tray of truffles to the food bank."

Sadie bit into a praline pecan truffle, contemplating Matteo's expression. He didn't look unwilling or even annoyed, but he was definitely uncertain and likely wondered what she was up to. After all, it wasn't anything she'd asked him to do before. Besides, this was his biggest sales period of the year, and he really didn't have extras to spare.

"This is really good with coffee!" Sadie exclaimed, completely off topic. Amber had brought her a "Sweetheart Latte" from Jay's Java Joint. The lightly cinnamon-laced drink complemented the praline flavor nicely.

"The food bank...," Matteo prompted.

"Right," Sadie said. She made herself focus. It was so easy to be distracted when in the presence of chocolate, not to mention chocolate and coffee combined. "The food bank. I'm planning to volunteer for their Valentine's Day breakfast."

A sly smile crossed Matteo's face. "Have they been warned?"

"Funny guy," Sadie said.

Matteo laughed. "You know I'm kidding. I've known you to be involved in community activities a few times without getting into trouble. Although there was that auction incident..."

"That wasn't my fault," Sadie protested. "I was just stretching!"

"And the thrift shop's sidewalk sale…"

Sadie sighed. "Again, not my fault. I forgot my reading glasses that day and misread the decimal point."

"What were those again? Oh, I remember now," Matteo said, much to Sadie's dismay. "Designer bracelets that were supposed to be five dollars each."

"In my defense, I contributed the extra four dollars and ninety-five cents for each one at the end of the day," Sadie said. He did have a point though. She should have thought over the price of those bracelets more carefully even though she thought she'd read the sign correctly. Five cents seemed too good to be true. She'd even bought a few for herself.

"Back to the truffles," Matteo said.

"Yes." Sadie cheered up, glad to see the subject switch back to the matter at hand.

"I'll have a box ready for you at the end of business today. I just need to make sure I fill all my customer orders first. How does that sound?"

"It sounds wonderful," Sadie said. "Thank you. And the food bank thanks you." She grabbed one more truffle from the sample tray and headed to the door.

"That remains to be seen," Matteo said.

"I heard that!" Sadie called back as she slipped out the door.

* * *

Amber, in between customers at the time Sadie walked into Flair, stood in front of the shop's long mirror, holding two hangers, one against her chest, the other held away.

"Can't decide?" Sadie took a stance next to her, tilting her head as she pondered the ivory blouse Amber currently debated. "Maybe too sophisticated for a lunch date," Sadie said. "Try the one in your other hand."

Switching arms, Amber held up a soft pink turtleneck. She scrunched up her shoulders and waited for Sadie's opinion.

"Appropriate for the holiday," Sadie admitted. "That's a definite maybe. Set it aside and think about it during the day."

"Good idea," Amber said. She hung the turtleneck on the hold rack near the sales counter as the front door chimed. As she greeted a single incoming customer, Sadie retreated to her back office to catch up on boutique paperwork.

"What do you think, Coco?" Sadie asked as she took Coco from her tote bag and let the Yorkie curl up on her lap. "Should we pay bills or order some scarves from Italy?"

Always one to voice an opinion in line with Sadie's, Coco propped her head on the edge of the desk and yipped.

"Good choice," Sadie said. "Scarves from Italy it is." She pulled a sales catalog from a corner stack and opened it to a bookmarked section. As she began to look over color and pattern choices, Amber poked her head in.

"Someone here to see you."

Sadie frowned. "Don't tell me it's someone who *hopped* on in unexpectedly."

"One and the same," Amber said, well aware of Sadie's nickname for the SFPD detective. "Should I send him back?"

"Better off here than out in the store." Sadie tapped her fingers on the scarf catalog as she waited for the detective to appear. Not even a minute later, he appeared in her office doorway. Sadie sighed. He could have at least browsed along the way, maybe found something for his wife. *No stopping a man on a mission.*

"Good morning, Ms. Kramer." Detective Frogert greeted Sadie and, without invitation, took a seat across the desk from her.

Sadie retaliated by lifting Coco up and placing her on the desktop to wander around as she pleased. Noting the detective shrink back in the chair, Sadie felt a sense of satisfaction, as if she'd pulled off an unexpected move on a chess player.

"I'm not fond of dogs, especially small ones," Frogert said.

Sadie nodded as if considering that as a serious statement. "Then I don't recommend getting one for your police station. Or at least I wouldn't put a Yorkie in your K-9 unit."

Straight-faced, Frogert ignored Sadie's sarcasm and got right to the point. "I could use your help."

Sadie, taken off guard, simply said, "You could." This came across as a vague statement, similar to the way one might say *Huh*.

Frogert waited for more of a response. He ran his hand across his forehead and set it on the edge of the desk. Sadie fought back the urge to applaud when Coco scooted right over and licked his hand. He removed his hand just as quickly as he'd placed it there. He shook it in the air as if trying to flick off an insect. Resigned, he placed it on the arm of his chair. Coco, appearing insulted, trotted back across the desk and jumped into Sadie's lap.

"And just how could I help you?" Sadie said as she stroked Coco's head with pride. A smile started to grow at the thought she was finally in the driver's seat. It faded quickly when she realized she didn't know what the vehicle was.

"We've narrowed our investigation," Frogert said. "We're focusing on one individual now. I believe we met at his office."

"Luke Manning?" *Well, obviously Luke Manning*, Sadie thought as soon as the name crossed her lips. *Zany Z's is hardly an office*. That hit Sadie from out of the blue. The police were focusing on one of the men? Not the women? Either she was way off track or they were clueless. Maybe some of each.

"Yes," Frogert said. "But this is confidential, you understand."

"Of course," Sadie said, not understanding in the least. "How is it you think I could help? I don't know him. I just stopped by his office that one time."

"But you mentioned your accountant recommended him," Frogert said.

"I did?" Now Sadie was truly baffled. She replayed discussions she'd had with the detective, trying to recall a conversation along those lines.

"Not to *me*," Frogert said, catching on to Sadie's confusion. "To Manning's receptionist, when you tried to see him."

"Oh, right," Sadie said, recalling the excuse she'd given for being there. "But how did you... Oh, never mind. Silly question." He was a detective, that's how he knew. He would have gone to the office to question why *she* had gone there. The receptionist would have relayed the short conversation she and Sadie had exchanged during that visit.

"I've made an appointment for you to see him," Frogert continued.

Sadie raised her eyebrows. "Isn't he out of town?"

"He was," Frogert said. "Now he's back from his fishing trip, and he's in the office today. I was able to get you in at four thirty."

"Today?" Sadie questioned whether or not she'd heard correctly.

Frogert nodded. "Yes, today. This is a murder investigation, as you know. Time is of the essence." He reached forward to place his hand on her desk for emphasis but thought better of it and pulled it back.

Time is of the essence? Who says that? Sadie gathered her thoughts. It was certainly short notice, and she didn't feel like she owed Froggy any favors, but the appointment could work to her advantage. She might find out more about the mysterious woman from his office. Or at least get some advice about a money market account she'd been considering.

"So are we set?" The detective leaned forward slightly, preparing to stand.

Sadie nodded. "Why not? Is there anything in particular you want me to ask him?"

This time Frogert stood. "I'll brief you outside when you get there."

"Why not brief me now?" Sadie frowned, uncomfortable about not having all the information up front.

"Because I want to be there anyway, for your protection," Frogert said. "Right now I need to go buy my wife some of Matteo's chocolate. Thank you for that reminder the other day."

Sadie stood after Frogert left. She placed Coco in the tote bag and grabbed her jacket. At least she could swing home and change into something worthy of a visit to the financial district before heading down there.

"I have an unexpected appointment," Sadie said as she stopped to see Amber on the way out. "Do you think you'll be fine for the afternoon?"

Amber nodded. "Definitely. Business is good, but not rushed."

Sadie looked around, noting only a couple of customers browsing. "Okay. Text me if you need anything."

"You look nervous," Amber said. "Are you sure you're fine?"

"Absolutely. Nothing to worry about," Sadie said. "It's just a little financial consultation, and Froggy will be there." She thanked Amber for covering and stepped outside.

Right. Froggy will be there. For my protection. Great, just great.

SEVENTEEN

Detective Frogert was already at the Stannon-Fielder building when Sadie arrived. His eyes widened slightly, and he nodded with approval as she walked up. This told her that wearing the conservative dress and jacket she usually reserved for bank meetings and funerals had been the right choice. The string of pearls had obviously been a good choice as well, as tempted as she'd been to wear her seasonal reindeer necklace with flashing red noses.

"Good afternoon," Frogert said formally as if he hadn't just seen her hours before. "I'll get right to the point."

"An excellent plan," Sadie quipped. The sooner the charade was over, the better. Coco, either in agreement or disturbed by the recognizable voice, yipped twice, causing Frogert to stare at Sadie's tote bag and frown. She smiled. "You were saying?"

Frogert cleared his throat. "Yes. We know your late husband was a well-known real estate developer and investor, so it won't seem odd that you're paying a visit to Manning Property Holdings."

"I see," Sadie said. Of course she saw. He'd done his homework. She'd started off as a person of interest, thanks to Gladys—er, Mags—the victim's nosy neighbor. "So what is it I'm meeting with him about?"

"It's very simple," Frogert said.

I doubt it, Sadie thought.

"You simply need to ask about possible investment

opportunities," Frogert continued.

"That's it?" *Piece of cake. Chocolate, preferably.*

"Yes, that and one more thing."

Sadie resisted the urge to sigh. She knew it had sounded too easy.

"Somewhere in the conversation, we need you to ask about his fishing trip."

Right. That'll fit right into a financial discussion with an advisor I've never met before.

"His fishing trip," Sadie repeated. "You want me to ask about his fishing trip? How do you suggest I work that little tidbit in? And do I get some sort of junior deputy badge for doing this? You know, like the national parks give out?"

"No," Frogert said flatly. "You can say your late husband was fond of fishing."

Sadie laughed. "Morris hated fishing."

Frogert's tone became impatient. "Mr. Manning won't know that. And you're being asked to help the SFPD here, which I'd consider an honor. So I wouldn't be so flippant."

Sadie straightened up quickly but only out of indignation, not because of the detective's insulting remark. She hardly considered being sent in to interrogate a murder suspect an honor.

"Just what do you want me to ask?"

"Mention something about Morris liking to try different fishing techniques, including those using nets of some sort."

Sadie's eyes lit up. "The murder weapon was a fishing net? The victim was strangled?" She practically beamed with excitement. *Great news!* Okay, not exactly great news for the victim, obviously, but a great clue.

Frogert stepped forward abruptly. "Ms. Kramer, please lower your voice. You know I can't divulge details about an ongoing investigation. I'm simply asking you to mention something in order to see how he reacts to the phrase."

"I understand," Sadie said. Froggy was really starting to get on her nerves. Now she just wanted to get the whole thing over with. "What time do you have, Detective?"

Frogert twisted his wrist and looked down at a basic but functional watch. "Four twenty-three. No, make that four twenty-four."

"Well, it's not polite to be late to an appointment." Sadie walked to the elevator and pushed the Up button. Frogert followed her.

"You feel comfortable with the assignment?"

Sadie watched the panel above the elevator door. The descending numerals were lighting up one by one, indicating the elevator was on its way down. She wasn't keen on the idea of the meeting itself, but leaving Froggy behind was appealing. "I wouldn't say comfortable is the right word, Detective," she said. "Informed, yes."

Much to Sadie's relief, the elevator bell chimed, the doors opened, and she stepped inside. Turning to face outward, she pushed the button for the seventeenth floor and was delighted to see the detective's face disappear as the sliding metal doors came together.

The ride to Manning Property Holdings passed quickly, thanks to the absence of other passengers. Stepping into the lobby, Sadie was struck with the feeling that the marble tiling seemed colder than on her first visit and the sparse décor even plainer. The ambiance of the place wasn't her style at all. If she really were interested in investing at the time, this wouldn't be a company she'd pick. She'd simply look around and walk out. In fact, that very idea seemed suddenly appealing. If not for Froggy waiting below, she would have done exactly that. Still, on the upside, he'd given her a perfect excuse to fish—she chuckled out loud at the play on words—for information. She wasn't about to pass that up.

"May I help you?" The same receptionist she'd encountered before looked up from the desk, an expression on her face that Sadie took as disapproval. Apparently, chuckling out loud was frowned upon at Manning Property Holdings, yet another reason to not give them her business.

"Yes, thank you," Sadie said. "I'm here to see Luke Manning."

"Do you have an appointment?"

In spite of herself, Sadie smirked. "Yes, I do." Coco yipped to back up her claim. Conveniently, the reception desk's intercom buzzed at the same time, muffling the tiny bark.

"Yes, Mr. Manning." After a brief pause, the receptionist continued. "Yes, I believe Ms. Kramer has just arrived." Another pause. "Yes, I'll tell her." She looked at Sadie with a forced smile. "He'll be right out."

"Thank you!" Sadie chirped cheerfully, simply to annoy the woman. She strolled over to an arrangement of photographs on the lobby wall, all boasting impressive structures with stunning backdrops of bay views and sunsets. She turned back toward the reception desk at the sound of footsteps approaching.

"Ms. Kramer?"

Sadie recognized Luke Manning immediately. At least the receptionist hadn't been lying before about him not being in. This was definitely the attractive man she'd seen leaving the building on her first visit. And he was just as attractive this time, right down to his firm, no-nonsense handshake and welcoming smile. Maybe she *would* give him some business after all. Unless he was the killer, of course. Then it would be out of the question.

"I'm pleased to meet you, Mr. Manning," Sadie said in her most business-worthy voice.

"Please call me Luke. Let's go to my office." Luke ushered Sadie down a hallway and into a spacious corner room. In contrast to the austere lobby, the office featured warm, rich colors, overstuffed chairs, and a spectacular view. Sadie felt immediately at home and even more certain he wasn't the killer. Whatever had caused Froggy to narrow the search in this direction was beyond her.

"I knew your late husband, Morris," Luke said. "I was sorry to hear he'd passed away."

That took Sadie by surprise, though she wasn't sure why. She didn't recall Morris mentioning Manning Property Holdings, but Morris had worked with dozens of companies. They'd rarely discussed his business dealings; they'd always made a point of keeping business and personal life separate. However, the unexpected remark on Luke's part gave Sadie the perfect opening right off the bat.

"Thank you," Sadie said, politely accepting the condolences. "Did you know him from business or fishing?"

Luke looked surprised but not uncomfortable in any way as she would expect a guilty person to be. Froggy would be disappointed. "I knew him from a deal over in the East Bay," he said. "I didn't know Morris liked to fish."

He didn't, Sadie thought to herself. "He just dabbled in it," she said aloud.

"Well, if I'd known that, I would have invited him along on the boat with us. We go out at least twice a month during the season."

"During the season?" Sadie repeated.

"Crab season," Luke said. "There's a group of us guys who get together."

"Ah," Sadie said. "Like a club for men, but with fishing poles?" It was a ridiculous comment, but it might lead to some detail that could come in handy.

Luke laughed. "Crab nets, not fishing poles. And some women go out on the trips too. Not many, but a few." He offered Sadie coffee or tea, which she politely declined, and then got down to business. "So tell me what I can do for you. The message I was given said you're looking into some type of investment."

"Yes," Sadie said. "But I don't know what exactly." *True statement indeed.* "Morris always handled those types of things. I just thought I'd touch base with you in case you know of anything coming up."

Luke ran through a variety of possibilities. Sadie nodded in what she hoped was a knowledgeable manner, repeating his phrases now and then for effect.

"Why don't I put together a proposal for you," Luke said. "I'll include a variety of options. We have another project forming in the East Bay, as well as several in Marin and Alameda counties. Give me about a week to prepare it, and then we can discuss whatever looks interesting to you."

Sadie smiled. "An excellent suggestion," she said. *And a good segue out of here.* She stood and thanked Luke for his time. He walked her out to the lobby where they parted ways, Luke returning to his office and Sadie preparing to meet Froggy. As expected, the detective was waiting for her across from the elevator when she stepped out.

"So, what did you find out?" Frogert said, getting right to the point.

"Nothing," Sadie said. "Well, that's not true. I believe I did learn something."

The detective's expression brightened slightly, at least as

much as his low-key personality allowed. "So," he repeated, "what did you find out?"

"There's a good investment possibility in the East Bay."

"What else," Frogert said impatiently, the bright expression gone.

"That you've got the wrong person." Sadie adjusted her tote bag on her shoulder. "Luke Manning isn't your killer. And now I really must get back to the shop. Good day, Detective."

EIGHTEEN

mber was in the process of closing up Flair when Sadie returned from the meeting with Luke Manning. The front door was locked, and some of the track lighting had been turned off already, but she could see Amber at the register inside.

Sadie used her key to open the door. Stepping inside, she heard the familiar sound of change dropping into the cash drawer. Knowing it never helped to be interrupted when counting money, she waved at Amber, who nodded in return while counting out loud in order to not lose track. Passing through the shop, Sadie continued to the back office.

"Here you go," she said as she took Coco out of her tote bag and placed her on the floor. Coco extended her front legs and pulled into a long stretch. She then reversed the motion to stretch her back legs. Sadie smiled, watching her. The dramatic stretches reminded her of some type of doggy yoga. She wouldn't put it past Coco to devise something clever like that. Perhaps Coco could even lead an outdoor class at the local bark park.

As Coco trotted out to greet Amber, Sadie turned her attention to a giant pink box on her desk. The Cioccolato logo flowed across the top in scrolled lettering. Peeking inside, she found a generous batch of truffles, along with a tiny note that simply said "no" with a smiley face. Sadie laughed. Matteo knew full well that she'd be tempted to sneak one for herself.

She closed the box, saving them all for the food bank.

Proud of her self-discipline, she walked to the front, where Amber was just finishing the register cash-out. The pink turtleneck still hung on the hold rack, a denim vest beside it. Sadie smiled, approving of the combination. The vest would tone down the pink of the turtleneck while still keeping a feminine touch to the outfit. It was a perfect combination for Amber's lunch date with Dylan.

"So, did you try one of the truffles in that box on your desk?" Amber asked. A sly smile accompanied the question.

"Of course not," Sadie said with mock indignation. "Those are for the food bank."

"Ah, okay then." Amber reached under the counter and pulled several papers from a printer.

"You look disappointed that I didn't try one," Sadie said. She handed Amber the stapler on the counter so she could consolidate and staple the sales reports together.

Amber smiled. "Of course I'm not. I just owe Matteo ten bucks now."

"Seriously?" Sadie laughed. "You two bet on whether or not I'd swipe one? And you bet *against me?*"

Coco, hearing the laughter, trotted over and yipped to join in. Sadie lifted her up on the counter and set her on her usual pillow.

"It wasn't a bet against you," Amber protested. "It was simply a guess based on your usual… er, lack of willpower around chocolate."

"Well, I'm not offended," Sadie said. "You know me well. I'm actually surprised Matteo bet that I wouldn't try one, though he did put that note inside to tweak my guilt if I did."

Amber stood up after signing the daily sales report. "What note?"

"Just a note that said 'no' with a funny little smiley face," Sadie said.

"That rat!" Amber exclaimed. "That's cheating. That nullifies the bet."

Sadie nodded. "That sounds fair to me. He swayed the odds in his favor."

"Exactly." Amber handed Sadie the printed reports, as well as a bag for the cash drop. "So what was this little errand that came up so suddenly after the detective left? You hurried out of here pretty quickly."

"I just hurried so I could get it over with and get back here," Sadie said as she headed to the office with the end-of-day paperwork and cash. "The errand wasn't my idea. Froggy wanted me to meet with one of the guys who sent Sue Bennett the Valentine's chocolates."

Amber lifted Coco from the pillow and followed Sadie. "I hope he didn't send you back to Zany Z's." She set Coco down on the floor and peeked inside the chocolate box, shaking her head at the note Matteo had cleverly placed inside.

"No," Sadie said. "I'm not sure I would have gone along with that. This was a meeting with the guy in the financial district."

"Ah." Amber nodded. "Hence the uptown attire you changed into. You weren't planning this meeting. How did it come up so suddenly?"

"Froggy took it upon himself to set it up as an investment consultation. Kind of him, don't you think?" Sadie said in a polished tone of sarcasm that she'd spent decades perfecting.

"Not especially," Amber said. "But knowing the way you think, you figured you'd get some information out of it or you would have refused to go."

Sadie laughed. "You know me well."

"So did you find anything out?"

"I think so," Sadie said. "I'm fairly sure now that Luke Manning isn't the killer. He seemed far too open when discussing fishing. Wait, not fishing, crabbing is more accurate."

Amber nodded. "Well, you lost me completely at 'fishing' but go on."

"Luke Manning had just returned from a fishing trip, according to Froggy." Sadie patted her lap, and Coco jumped up, settling in comfortably. "So my assignment—if you could call it that—was to ask him about investment possibilities and question him about the fishing trip to see if he acted oddly."

"And I take it he didn't," Amber said.

"Not at all," Sadie said. "In fact, he was excited to talk about it, including a group he belongs to that goes out on crabbing excursions. He wouldn't make those references if he were trying to hide something."

"Like the fact he might have killed someone."

"Yes," Sadie said. "Or what he might have used, which I think I now know."

Amber sat down as if expecting to hear something shocking or disturbing.

"I think poor Sue Bennett was strangled," Sadie said. "Froggy practically admitted it. At least he didn't deny it. He just gave me that 'can't comment on an ongoing investigation' excuse when I suggested she was strangled with a fishing net of some sort. I mean, it seems obvious to me. Otherwise, he'd have no reason to suspect Luke Manning."

"But the other two men had access to fishing nets," Amber said. "That guy at Fisherman's Wharf must be around them every day."

"Yes, and Zany Z's has them on the walls," Sadie added.

"But also…" Her voice trailed off as she thought back to the rest of the crazy bar's décor. She turned to the office computer and typed a few words into the search engine. "Look at this."

Amber stepped around the desk and looked over Sadie's shoulder at some images on the screen. "What are those?"

"Crab nets," Sadie said. "This is what Luke Manning was talking about. They use these for amateur crabbing." She tilted her head sideways as a whimsical thought hit her. "Or I suppose you could flip it upside down and use it as a hat. Not much good in the rain with all those holes in the netting."

"Or for a planter," Amber said. "That's what it looks like to me. You know those hanging baskets that you see at the garden center—a wire basket hanging from a rope."

"Yes." Sadie leaned closer to the screen as Coco yipped in protest at being squished. "A rope… that's it." She sat back and looked at Amber. Coco let out a dramatic sigh of relief.

"That's what?" Amber patted Coco on the head in sympathy.

"The murder weapon wasn't a net," Sadie said. "Sue Bennett was strangled with a *rope*, the kind that holds a crab net."

"You're positive?" Amber raised an eyebrow.

"*Almost* positive," Sadie said, tapping one finger against her chin. "It makes sense. All the suspects had access to that type of rope. They had the means to commit the crime."

"So you're talking about the kind of rope that Luke Manning uses on his group's crabbing excursions," Amber said.

"Also the kind Bruno has easy access to down at the wharf," Sadie added.

"And…" Amber waited for Sadie to finish the thought, which she quickly did.

"Yes, the kind hanging from the ceiling at Zany Z's place," Sadie said.

"But there are all sorts of ropes," Amber pointed out. "How

can you be sure it was the kind used for crabbing?"

"I can't without confirmation from Froggy," Sadie said. "And he's not going to give me that kind of detail. But..." She stood, holding Coco against her chest while she collected her tote bag and jacket. "I think I know how to find out for sure."

"I know that look," Amber said as she watched Sadie gather her things. "Just go. I'll lock up the shop."

"Thanks," Sadie said, already heading for the front door with one arm in a jacket. "And that denim vest with the turtleneck is perfect," she called back over her shoulder. Balancing Coco, her tote, and the box of truffles, she headed for her car.

NINETEEN

The San Francisco Bay looked especially exquisite from Sadie's penthouse windows. She admired the view as she sipped sparkling water with a slice of lime. The lights along the waterfront seemed like signals that she was on the right track.

Moving to the sofa, she took a seat, glad to be sporting a comfy purple chenille bathrobe with turquoise piping around the edges. Upon her arrival home, she'd practically thrown the box of truffles on the kitchen counter in her eagerness to get out of the stuffy outfit she'd worn to Luke Manning's office. Coco had landed on the floor more gently, where she now batted around her red lobster toy.

Sadie set her sparkling water on a side table, the Waterford crystal glass reflecting light from a chandelier above. She picked up the phone, pausing only briefly to collect her thoughts before dialing Broussard's number.

"Ms. Kramer."

"Detective Broussard."

Sadie smiled. The formal greetings they exchanged never lost their flirtatious appeal.

"How are you this fine evening?" Broussard said.

"Quite entertained, actually," Sadie said. "It's been an interesting day." She took a sip of sparkling water, not entirely sure how to fill Broussard in on the events of the day. He wasn't likely to be thrilled with Froggy's latest scheme.

"In what way?" Broussard's voice sounded hesitant, unsure he wanted to hear the answer. "You're still chasing down those suspects in the Bennett murder case, aren't you? Go ahead and fill me in. I've been following the case closely. I won't get upset. I'd rather know what's going on than not know."

We'll see about that, Sadie thought. "I made a visit to Luke Manning's office today."

"You what?" Broussard practically shouted into the phone.

So much for not getting upset. "In my defense, it wasn't my idea," Sadie said. "Froggy set the appointment up."

This time Broussard was silent, which Sadie knew wasn't a good sign. She could sense him fuming on the other end of the line. She was almost thankful for the miles between San Francisco and New Orleans. She'd bet Froggy would be even more thankful.

"Detective Frogert sent you into a murder suspect's office?" Broussard said when he was finally calm enough to speak.

"Well, yes," Sadie said. "But it was under very believable pretenses: to ask about investment opportunities. It's something I do on occasion anyway. I handle my late husband's portfolio, so I try to stay current on upcoming possibilities."

"I doubt that's the reason he sent you in."

"Okay, not exactly," Sadie admitted. "But it was a perfect cover."

"A 'cover,' you say?" To Sadie's relief, Broussard laughed. "I must have missed the part where you went to the police academy and became an undercover cop."

Now Sadie smiled. She spoke fluent sarcasm and could appreciate a good jab. Besides, his lighter mood provided an opening for the trick she'd planned.

"Did you know the murder weapon was a rope from a crabbing net?" Sadie waited for Broussard's response, which came quickly.

"How did you find that out?" Broussard said. "I can't believe Frogert released that information to you."

Sadie smiled. *Thank you, Detective Broussard.*

"It surprised me as well," Sadie said. "Especially the part about the crab net."

"He went into that much detail? I'm surprised," Broussard said.

Coco brought the red lobster toy over to Sadie and dropped it at her feet. "No, I figured that out on my own," Sadie said. "You might be surprised to know I've done a little detective work myself in the past, academy or no academy." She smirked as she tossed Coco's toy gently into the center of the room. Of course Broussard knew that already.

"You don't say," Broussard quipped. "I never would have guessed it." *More sarcasm.* She continued to admire the handsome New Orleans detective more and more.

"Actually, I'm not sure Froggy connects the rope with crabbing," Sadie said. "I'm sure they did tests on the rope and found salt water. I mean, that's what they would have done, right?"

"True," Broussard said. "We always run forensic tests on articles found at the scene, anything that might be a clue. Obviously, suspected murder weapons are included in that."

"Well, there wouldn't have been an actual crab net there, I don't think..." Sadie's voice trailed off as she contemplated that. "Wait," she said suddenly. "There might have been, after all." Luke Manning's description of his crabbing group came back to her. When she'd flippantly referred to it as a boys' club, he'd said that a few women went out on the crabbing excursions as well. Could that be where he'd met Sue Bennett? Where *all* the men had met her?

"Sadie?" Broussard's voice interrupted her thoughts,

bringing her back to the discussion at hand. She'd nearly forgotten she was in the middle of a conversation.

"A common interest!" Sadie said. "That's it!" She picked up the red lobster toy, which had landed at her feet again, and waved it around in the air like a flag at a parade. Coco sat nearby, tapping her paw impatiently.

"That's what?" Broussard said. Sadie could tell he was puzzled just by his tone.

"That's where the men who sent the chocolate all knew her from," Sadie said. "I'd bet on it." Why hadn't she thought of that before? Not the crabbing "club" in particular, if it could be called that, but the idea that there could be a common interest that led to Sue being wooed by the three men. The fact that the men were so different from one another had struck Sadie as odd before, but not important. As the saying went, each to his own—or, more appropriately at the moment, to *her* own. But in this case, the common interest *was* important after all. It was intricately tied to the method of the crime.

"I'm almost afraid to ask, but what's going on in that inquisitive mind of yours right now? You've been quiet."

"Is quiet a bad thing?" Sadie said, stalling as she pulled her new theory together.

"Exactly what I'm trying to figure out at the moment." Again, Sadie could tell Broussard was smiling.

"I couldn't come up with a connection between the three men and the victim before," Sadie explained. "The men are so completely different from each other. I'm rather disappointed in myself that I didn't consider a common hobby."

"Sometimes the link between victim and suspects can be unexpected," Broussard said. "It's one of the reasons we have to dig deeper into backgrounds rather than draw conclusions based on the scene itself. It's actually a good thing those men all sent her chocolate."

Sadie laughed. "Well, of course, that's always a good thing."

"You know what I mean," Broussard said. "It provided some leads that, short of fingerprints—trustworthy—and reports from that nosy neighbor—not trustworthy—the police were able to follow and are still following, obviously."

"I think they're still missing the boat." Sadie couldn't help herself; she burst out laughing at the accidental pun.

"And just what boat would that be?" Broussard asked.

"The figurative boat," Sadie said.

"You've lost me now."

"The women," Sadie explained.

"Ah, not the crabbing boat," Broussard said. "What sort of boat do you mean?"

"I'm still trying to figure it out, but there are quite a few possibilities."

"For example?"

"Well, there's the anger boat, the jealousy boat, the revenge boat…"

"Okay, okay," Broussard said. "I see your point. You could be right, as much as I hate to admit it."

"Painful?" Sadie teased. "Admitting I might be a step ahead of the SFPD? Maybe they just don't understand women well enough."

Broussard chuckled. "I'm not sure anyone does."

"Ha," Sadie said. "On that note, I think I'm going to relax with a good mystery book and get my mind off this for a while." *Or at least try to.*

"Excellent idea."

"Good night, Detective Broussard."

"Good night, Ms. Kramer."

TWENTY

Sadie eyed the box of truffles on the kitchen counter. Would it hurt to have just one little nibble with her morning coffee? It was a dilemma she often faced in the presence of chocolate. But this was different. These were intended for the food bank. Gathering every available ounce of willpower, she dropped wheat bread in the toaster and turned away from the temptation.

A yip from Coco served as a reminder that she wasn't the only one expecting a nibble of something to start the day. Reaching into a cupboard reserved for dog food and treats, she pulled out Coco's favorite kibble and poured it into an artsy bowl they'd acquired at the French Market in New Orleans. Setting it down with a second bowl of fresh water alongside it, Sadie turned back to the toaster just as the golden slices of wheat toast popped up.

Spreading an ample amount of butter on the toast—after all, she had to compensate for foregoing the chocolate—she took a seat at the kitchen table and sent a text to Amber. "Happy Valentine's Day," she typed between sips of coffee and munches of toast. She reminded Amber that she'd be at the food bank when Flair opened but would return in plenty of time to cover the shop while Amber went on her lunch date with Dylan.

Dressing for holidays had always been a tradition for Sadie, even when she was a child. This had often been a source of embarrassment for her poor mother as well as teasing at school. But festive occasions called for festive wardrobe, as far as Sadie was concerned. It was one fashion tradition she'd carried on since those early years.

"Come, Coco," Sadie said after setting her toast dish and coffee mug in the kitchen sink. "Let's see what we can come up with for today."

Sadie's walk-in closet was a universe unto itself. Truth be told, it was intended by the architect to be a bedroom situated next to the master bedroom. But a simple addition of a door between the two rooms during a remodel turned it into a closet fit for... well, an eccentric, fashion-crazy boutique owner.

Two walls featured long racks for hanging clothing, each at different levels to accommodate clothing of varying lengths. Low dressers flanked the wall with a higher rack above them for blouses, jackets, and other items that didn't require a length of space below.

A third wall sported shelving and cubbyholes for folded sweaters and shoes. And more shoes and, in days gone by, even more shoes: high heels, pumps, and upscale footwear appropriate for social events that she and her late husband had attended. Sadie had taken to preferring flats these days for comfort and practicality. This simpler approach to footwear had kept her assortment of choices down to a mere four dozen, enough to include most colors, animal prints, metallic tones, and a sizable collection of fluffy slippers—some, but not all, with bunny ears or other frivolous designs.

The fourth wall's fixtures split off to two sides, the door to her bedroom situated in the middle. One side consisted of a dresser for scarves and a conglomeration of fixtures above for jewelry and accessories. The other, of course, was reserved for

Coco's own wardrobe and accessories: coats, collars, leashes, and bows, all assorted by colors and stored on hangers and shelves shaped like dog bones. A fluffy pink dog bed rested on the floor below the assortment, a doghouse shaped mirror next to it. This allowed Coco a place to contemplate her preferences and to approve or veto options.

Sadie's counterpart to Coco's fluffy dog bed was a circular Victorian sofa that she picked up at an auction. The burgundy velvet and walnut bench graced the center of the room. Sitting there now, she patted the seat, and Coco hopped up to sit beside her. Together, they debated options for the day.

"Whatever we pick must be very sweet," Sadie mused. "After all, it *is* Valentine's Day. We must dress accordingly." Coco yipped in agreement. "And cheerful," Sadie added, thinking the food bank patrons would appreciate a festive touch, as would her own boutique's customers when she arrived at the store. "Red, I think," Sadie said. "You have a red collar, Coco."

Coco jumped off the velvet bench and trotted over to her mini-closet area. Sadie followed and watched as Coco pawed through a basket of accessories. Knowing dogs didn't see colors the same way humans did, she knew "collar" was the word Coco was following.

"This one is perfect," Sadie said as she reached into the basket and pulled out a sparkling red rhinestone collar. "And you have a matching leash for that one too. All you'll need is a heart-shaped bow on your head." Coco tilted her head to the side and looked quizzically at Sadie. "Up to you," Sadie said. Coco let out a sound resembling more of a huff than her usual yip. "Okay, just the collar and leash it is," Sadie said. The day promised to be full of challenges as it was; there was no use starting it by arguing with a Yorkie.

She replaced Coco's regular pink collar with the sparkling

red one and set the matching leash aside for when they went out. "Coco," she explained gently, "we're going to leave your hot pink iPod Shuffle home. You can get by without your favorite salsa playlist for today. I promise you can wear it for Cinco de Mayo as well as some nonholiday excursions between now and then."

Moving to her own wardrobe section, Sadie considered her options. Normally she would pick something fanciful for the boutique ambiance. But she'd be at the food bank for the first part of the morning. With her luck, she'd end up spilling something on herself. She did tend to be clumsy on occasion. This was yet another reason she'd given up the less-practical and balance-altering shoes.

"Let's go with this," Sadie said, pulling a red chenille sweater from one of the cubbyholes. It was just elegant enough to fit the holiday, and she hadn't worn it since Christmas. "And how about pink slacks—not exactly practical but appropriately festive for the holiday, don't you think?" She looked to her sidekick for a second opinion. Coco simply licked her paw and smoothed back a wayward strand of fur.

Sadie donned the two main wardrobe items and then rummaged through a drawer of accessories specifically for holidays. Bypassing a giant pumpkin brooch and an electric garland of holiday lights, she pulled out a strand of large heart-shaped beads. She'd been delighted to find them at a local craft fair. Each bead was designed to look like a Valentine's Day heart candy. "Kiss me," "Hot stuff," "Cutie pie," and "Be mine" were among other traditional sayings. One bead with the words "Text me" served as a reminder that time marches on. She never would have seen that in a mixture when she was younger. Two matching candy-heart-shaped earrings—"True love" and "Yours 4Ever"—picked up the theme of the necklace. She put the whimsical accessories on along with red metallic flats. Standing in front of the dressing room's full-length mirror, she felt assured the outfit was complete.

Returning to the kitchen, Sadie found a text from Amber on her phone. *Arrived at the shop early. Strange note on the door. Thought I should warn you.*

Sadie frowned and typed back. *"Mrs. Jacobs? Her order will be in next week. I explained that to her. Always impatient."*

Setting the phone down on the counter, Sadie pulled a jacket from the hall closet and returned to check for another text.

No, unfortunately.

"Coco, what could be more unfortunate than a disgruntled customer?" The Yorkie simply blinked.

What then? Amber was already typing her answer, as indicated on the text screen, but Sadie felt impatient. She needed to get to the food bank in time to scope out the situation. She expected at least one, if not all three, of the women to show up.

Back off.

Sadie paused. That didn't sound at all like Amber. Oh, wait. *The note said that?*

Afraid so, Amber answered.

What kind of writing?

No writing.

Well, that didn't make sense. Unless…

Typed?

Little dots on the phone indicated Amber was typing back. *Cutout letters, like from a magazine.*

"You have got to be kidding," Sadie said out loud. "Coco,

someone has definitely been reading too many detective novels." Coco, ever happy to please, simply looked at Sadie, head tilted. It didn't matter that Coco didn't understand the words. She was always willing to back Sadie up. An admirable canine trait that Sadie never took for granted.

Sadie sighed. *Leave it on my desk,* she typed. *Thanks.* She placed the phone in a side pocket of her tote bag and helped Coco settle onto the velvet cushion inside.

"Let's go, Coco," she said. "We'll deal with the note when we get to the store."

TWENTY-ONE

arking spaces near the food bank were nonexistent, as was typical for San Francisco. She paid the necessary fee at a lot a block away and slung her tote over her shoulder. Holding the box of truffles carefully, she headed for her destination.

The one-block walk to the food bank was an eye-opener, even though Sadie was well aware of the varied neighborhoods in the city. The row of check-cashing storefronts, boarded-up shop windows with glass below them, and liquor stores with flashing neon signs gave her pause. She knew she led a privileged life and didn't take it for granted. But the scene that surrounded her as she maneuvered the trash-ridden sidewalk was a reality check.

She found the entrance to Free Harvest situated next to a bar with the mixed sounds of billiards and blaring music flowing from the door. A man in his fifties leaned against the wall outside, lighting a cigarette. His clothing looked decent, but his voice was ragged and harsh.

"Can't smoke inside," he said. Taking a drag, he coughed as he waved Sadie toward the door. She nodded and stepped inside.

The interior of Free Harvest was nicer than she expected, although it occurred to her that she hadn't known what to expect at all. The space was fairly large, adequate to house several long rows of tables that ran the length of the room.

A well-meaning attempt had been made to decorate for the holiday. Construction paper hearts dotted the center stretch of the tables, and streamers of red crepe paper dangled off to each side at periodic intervals.

"Over here." Sadie turned toward the voice, which was coming from the direction of a length of tables that ran perpendicular to the others. Aluminum pans rested end to end. A few large baskets sat at one end. Large drink dispensers loomed near the baskets. Several hairnet-wearing women—none that Sadie recognized—busied themselves bringing food from a kitchen just behind the serving tables.

"I'm Nora," the woman said. "Looks like you brought in a donation?"

"Yes," Sadie said as she approached.

"Pastry maybe?" Nora said, eyeing the pink box. It was a reasonable assumption, seeing as it was a breakfast event.

"Not exactly," Sadie said. She lifted the cardboard edge so the woman could see inside.

"Ah! Quite a treat!" Nora exclaimed, peeking inside. "I dare say we should save that for tonight's dinner. Chocolate and scrambled eggs might be a strange combination."

Sadie had to agree. As much as she felt chocolate was appropriate for any occasion, this could very well be an exception. "Where should I put these? I can help as well, if you can use me." Why not? Detective work and volunteering did not have to be mutually exclusive.

Nora nodded toward the kitchen door. "In there will be fine. And we're short volunteers today if you can stay. Go on back. Luke will give you an apron."

Luke? No, it couldn't be. There were plenty of Lukes in the world, right?

Stepping sideways to make way for a platter of sausage

coming through the door, Sadie waited until the way was clear and then entered.

The kitchen was small but functional. Shelving covered the left wall, two ovens and a range top stretched across the back wall, and a basic sink stood off to the right. The center of the room featured a spacious prep table where a man was pouring maple syrup from a large plastic jug into a serving pitcher. Even dressed in jeans, T-shirt, and an SF Giants baseball cap, rather than his professional attire, Sadie knew it was Luke Manning.

"Sadie Kramer," Luke said after looking over his shoulder to see who had entered. "What a nice surprise to see you here." He eyed the distinctive Cioccolato box she carried, but just as with the fishing conversation, he didn't seem to react oddly. "It looks like you're dropping off some pastries for today's breakfast?"

"Yes. I mean, no," Sadie said. "Not pastries, but truffles. Matteo, my next-door neighbor, makes amazing chocolate. My business neighbor, that is."

Luke nodded as he twisted the lid on the gallon maple syrup container. "I recognized the logo. I've used his shop to send gifts to clients on occasion."

Clients? Sadie took a mental double take as she set the box of chocolates down on the center table. Was it possible Sue Bennett was a client of Manning Property Holdings? Not a romantic interest? She felt like kicking herself. That hadn't even occurred to her. What kind of amateur detective was she anyway?

"That's a great gift for clients," Sadie said, at a loss for anything else to say.

"Yes. Personal, but not too personal," Luke said. "My fiancée suggested it."

Sadie nodded. "I might just drop a hint to my financial advisor. An excellent suggestion by your fiancée, I might say."

Luke laughed. "She's addicted to that place. I've never been there. I'm not much of a chocolate fan myself. She's busy today but will be here tonight to help with dinner."

"Speaking of helping, I met Nora out front. She said I could get an apron back here. I thought I'd stay and help out. And… where could I stash my bag?"

Luke grabbed an apron off one of the shelves, handed it to Sadie, and tilted his head toward the back of the kitchen. "There's a closet in that corner. Your bag will be safe in there."

Sadie thanked Luke for the apron and proceeded to situate her tote bag in the closet, whispering to Coco that she'd be back soon. She closed the door securely, returned to the center table, and put the apron on.

"We're short volunteers this morning, though we'll have plenty tonight," Luke said. "That pitcher of syrup goes in the middle of the buffet table. I have trays of pancakes keeping warm in the oven. He glanced at a clock. "People will start showing up soon."

"How many do you expect?"

"We could have anywhere from fifty to two hundred," Luke said. "We never know for sure. If we have too much food, we send some home with people. If we run out, well, there's nothing we can do. But the regulars know to show up early."

Sadie glanced around the kitchen before heading to the door. "It's amazing you can manage this by yourself."

"Oh, I just volunteer one day a week, plus an occasional holiday like this. And I'm not usually alone back here. I sometimes have one other person to help in the kitchen, but…" Luke's voice trailed off, and his face clouded over. "She's not with us anymore." He cleared his throat and moved to the range top, where a large kettle simmered. "Could you see if Nora's ready for this pot of oatmeal while you're out there? Thanks."

"Of course," Sadie said. She scooted out the door, set the syrup pitcher on the table, and looked around. A few early birds had shown up, undoubtedly the regulars Luke had mentioned. They'd staked out places at the tables and were drinking coffee from institution-type mugs.

"We always put the coffee out first," Nora explained. "It's something warm for them, plus it gives us time to set up the serving area without the crunch of a line."

"A very respectful crowd," Sadie said at the same time noting a familiar figure entering. It had only been a hunch that the women would show up, but so far her hunch was… dead on? No, poor use of the phrase, whether applicable or not.

"Absolutely," Nora said, nodding. "More respectful than some crowds I've seen at a few fancy restaurants." She checked plates and silverware beside a tall stack of trays.

"You're right about that," Sadie agreed, recalling more than one scene where demanding patrons chastised servers for errors that weren't their fault or slid money to maître d's in attempts to be catered to over others. There were times she and Morris had been embarrassed to be in the same room with hoity-toity customers behaving like that.

"I almost forgot," Sadie said. "Luke asked if you're ready for the oatmeal."

Nora looked up. "Oh, great, Lila's here! Yes, he can bring the oatmeal out now. There are two of us to serve—actually three, counting you."

"Happy to help," Sadie said, realizing it was true. Ulterior motives or not, she was participating in something worthwhile. It felt good.

"Sorry I'm late," Lila shouted without looking over. "It was a late night, as always. I'll be right out." She zoomed into the kitchen and reappeared a minute later, tying an apron around her waist. The pale floral print was an odd match for her Led Zepplin T-shirt.

"I'll get the oatmeal," Sadie said, returning to the kitchen. She grabbed two hot pads and carefully lifted the pot of oatmeal off the stove.

"Wait. I know you," Lila said bluntly as Sadie returned.

"Maybe," Sadie said evasively. "You look familiar too."

"At Flair," Lila said. "You were working there the other day."

Sadie nodded. It was both intriguing and informative that Lila seemed to think she was just a shop employee.

"And you were at Zany Z's recently too, weren't you?" Lila continued. "I thought you looked familiar when I saw you at Flair. That's why."

"Guilty as charged," Sadie said. She set the pot of oatmeal down in the serving area, ignoring Nora's raised eyebrows at the mention of the sleazy bar.

Luke appeared with a rectangular metal serving tray of pancakes and then made a second trip with another batch. Scrambled eggs followed. As the food built on the tables, so did the line of hungry customers, who eagerly held out trays and plates as Nora, Lila, and Sadie served up the hot breakfast of pancakes, eggs, and sausage. One by one, grateful men and women passed through the line until only a few remained.

"Any orange juice today?"

"Not today, Harold, sorry," Nora said to a man who was clearly a regular. "We hope to have some next Sunday."

"I'll be here," the man said, flashing a toothless grin.

Sadie watched him walk away and turned to Nora. "Is there usually orange juice?"

"When we can," Nora said. "We operate on donations. Sometimes it covers everything we want to serve, other times it doesn't. We have to make choices."

"I see," Sadie said, somehow feeling especially disappointed that Harold wouldn't have orange juice with his breakfast. It was a little thing in some ways, but in other ways, it wasn't.

A commotion in the kitchen interrupted Sadie's thoughts. At the sound of Luke's raised voice, Nora handed the spatula over to Sadie to continue dishing out pancakes while she checked to see what was going on. Sadie could hear Nora gasp as she opened the door to the kitchen. As Sadie placed a pancake on the plate of the last woman in line, she saw a blur of fur fly out into the room.

With a sinking feeling in her stomach, she handed the spatula to Lila and took off into the crowded dining area. Following the bobbing heads of the formerly calm crowd, Sadie frantically peered under tables but saw no sign of the culprit. Hearing laughter, she stood and glanced toward the enthusiastic sound. To her dismay, she zeroed in on the source of the entertainment. In the center of a particularly crowded table, Coco stood on her hind legs like a circus dog. Sadie made a beeline for the table.

"Here you go, doggie!" a man with a scruffy beard called out. He broke off a piece of sausage and tossed it in the air. Teetering on her hind paws, Coco caught the tasty morsel like a champ. Applause broke out, and another person at the table repeated the offering. Again, Coco snapped up the treat in midair. Even more applause filled the room. Torn between letting the show go on and taking the responsible route of stopping it, Sadie got the necessary nudge in the form of a voice by her side.

"Sadie!" Nora said, her voice a mix of sympathy and dismay. "Is that your dog?"

Meekly Sadie nodded. "I'm sorry. She was in my bag, in the closet, with the door closed. I don't understand how she got out."

"Lila never closes the closet door," Nora said. "She must have left it open when she put her purse in there. And, as much as the crowd loves this exhibition, we're going to be in deep syrup if a health inspector stops in."

"Understood," Sadie said. "I'll get her." She made a move for the table in an attempt to put an end to the show. But seeing Sadie reaching for her, Coco's mischievous side took over. She set off down the center of the long stretch of tables, finally stepping in a plate of butter and skidding off the end. She landed on the floor, a pancake balanced perfectly on her head. The crowd roared in appreciation, a sentiment not entirely shared by the volunteer staff.

"I'm so sorry," Sadie said, apologizing once she had Coco firmly held against her chest with one buttery arm. She plucked a morsel of sausage out of Coco's fur. "I'll just get my things and go. The box in the kitchen is full of truffles for anyone who wants a bite of chocolate."

"I could use some about now," Nora said, a smile forming. "But we'll save them for the dinner tonight."

"She's a cute little thing," Lila said. "I especially liked the way she modeled that pancake hat. Maybe that could be a new item for that shop you work in."

"Who knows?" Sadie said lightly. "Fashion trends change all the time."

"I'll start clean-up," Lila said, heading off toward the kitchen.

"I should really be helping," Sadie said. "But…"

Nora reached out and patted Coco on the head. "I think you'll have enough cleaning up to do when you get home. Seems you're taking some Valentine's breakfast home with you.

We'll take a rain check on the clean-up help. Maybe you could come by tonight if you don't have plans. We could always use an extra hand or two. Many vendors will be dropping off donations. Volunteers get to eat as well.

"Yes," Lila said. "Zane and I bring extra food from the bar whenever possible. Better than having it spoil."

"Actually, I'm not busy tonight," Sadie said. "I think I could come back."

"Maybe *just* you," Nora added as she glanced down at Coco and smiled.

"I'm the first to agree, trust me," Sadie said. "I'll grab my tote bag and apologize to Luke." She looked down at Coco, who bore what seemed like a feigned innocent look. "And you and I will have a little talk when we get home, understood?"

Coco sighed and dropped her head on Sadie's arm dramatically.

"Exactly," Sadie said.

A tiny whimper of apology followed.

TWENTY-TWO

Sadie stopped at home on the way to Flair, just long enough to give Coco a quick scrub-down in the bathroom sink.

"You could use a full grooming session, you little rascal, but at least you're presentable now." Sadie held the red rhinestone collar as she ran the blow-dryer over the Yorkie's fur. Coco raised her head and closed her eyes, enjoying the treatment. She'd always been fond of the blow-dryer's warm air. Of course, the extra attention from Sadie didn't hurt either.

Fortunately, Coco's shenanigans hadn't ruined Sadie's carefully chosen outfit for the day. She adjusted her candy heart necklace back below the neckline of her sweater, having tossed it over her shoulder while removing the butter and syrup from Coco's fur.

"Let's go," Sadie said, scooping Coco up and placing her in the tote bag. "We promised Amber we'd cover so she can have lunch with Dylan." *Finally*, Sadie added to herself. The flirtation between the two had gone on for months. They needed to spend some time together that didn't involve signing for incoming UPS packages.

With that in mind, Sadie headed for the shop. It was bound to be a busy shopping day in any case. Aside from covering Amber's lunch break, she wanted to be there to help customers. And there was the matter of the weird note left on the door as well.

Flair was busy when she arrived at the store. She stashed her jacket and tote bag in the back office and carried Coco up to the front to assume her rightful place on the counter pillow. The sparkling red collar worked well as an accent to Amber's hand lotion display, picking up the festive ribbons on the bottles. As an added bonus, the fragrance of the lotion covered any remaining scent of butter or sausage that Coco's quick clean-up might have missed.

"I'm worried about that note I found on the door," Amber whispered between customers at the register. "I hope you're not in danger."

"I'll call Froggy as soon as it slows down," Sadie said. "I don't want you worrying. This is an important day for you."

Amber blushed, and Sadie was charmed by the girl's reaction. *Ah, to be young again!* Sadie thought. Until she remembered the turmoil of young adulthood and dating, and her view became more sympathetic.

Sadie glanced at Amber and smiled. "You look lovely, by the way. I like the soft curls in your hair, as well as the denim headband. It picks up the blue of your vest." A yip followed, and Sadie turned to Coco. "Yes, you look lovely too, little one. And you're due for some lovely behavior to make up for this morning."

"Uh-oh, what did she do this time?" Amber laughed.

"Just a few antics on top of the food bank tables, that's all."

"On the serving table?" Amber raised her eyebrows and shot Coco a disapproving look.

"No, thank goodness," Sadie said. "But she did make a spectacle of herself on one of the customer tables, not that they minded. Honestly, I think she brought some cheer to the occasion."

"Good thing there were no health inspectors there," Amber said.

"Yes, those were the exact sentiments of the people who run the place."

The personal conversation paused in order to ring up several purchases from frantic, last-minute shoppers, all men. Jewelry, sweaters, and scarves all left with festive tissue paper and ribbon stuffed inside bags with store logos. It was amazing how fancy a paper bag could become with the right amount of decorative flourish.

Taking advantage of a break in activity, Sadie took Coco and moved to her office. She set Coco down and took a seat behind her desk. There, carefully set aside from other papers, was the odd note that Amber had found on the front door.

"At least the person could have used some colorful letters, Coco," Sadie said as she looked down at the note. "All black and white is so boring, especially on a holiday like this, don't you think? At least some pink."

"Or red," a familiar voice added. Sadie looked up to see Detective Frogert standing in the doorway. "Or maybe a combination of both," he added.

"Good morning, Detective," Sadie said. "I was just about to call you."

"Is that so?" Frogert stepped into the office and walked over to Sadie's desk. He looked down at the note and frowned. "I assume this is why you were planning to call me? Not simply to wish me a happy Valentine's Day."

Sadie attempted a smile. "No, Detective Frogert. Sorry to disappoint you, but I was not calling to wish you a happy Valentine's Day. I was indeed calling—or about to call—to discuss this note."

"When did you find it?" Frogert pulled a plastic glove from

his pocket and put it on. He picked up the note carefully by one corner and held it up to the light.

"I didn't find it," Sadie said. "Amber did. She's up at the register now. She said it was taped to the front door when she arrived to open the shop this morning."

Frogert nodded. He turned the paper over and inspected the back. "So it was left there sometime this morning or last night?"

"Of course," Sadie said. "It certainly wasn't there when we closed up last night. We would have noticed."

"Naturally," Frogert said. "I just have to ask questions, you know."

Well, ask something important then. Sadie was beginning to feel miffed. It had already been a long morning, and much of the day still loomed ahead.

"I'll take this down to the station to check for prints." Frogert pulled a large plastic baggie from his other pocket and dropped the note inside. "I assume yours will be on it?"

"I'm sure Amber's prints will be on it," Sadie said. "She's the one who found it and brought it in. But I haven't touched it. You conveniently showed up just as I was about to."

"Whoever put it there probably used gloves," Frogert said. "But it's worth checking." He sealed the top of the plastic bag and looked at Sadie. "Do you have any idea who might have left this for you? Have you received any threats—phone calls, other notes, anything like that?"

Sadie shook her head. "Nothing like that," she said. "I would have reported it if I had." *You've been the only one to bug me so far...*

"I'll get back to you later today," Frogert said. "Meanwhile, I would advise you to be careful. Watch for any strangers hanging around your place. Don't go out alone. Better yet, don't go out at all."

"I'm not going to live in fear, Detective," Sadie said sternly. "I have plans to help at Free Harvest's Valentine's dinner tonight. I was at their breakfast this morning, and it seems they could use extra help."

"Aha," Frogert said, nodding his head as if he'd just discovered some sort of giant government secret. "I knew it."

"Knew what?"

"That you were following Luke Manning," Frogert said. "I'm well aware that he is a volunteer there. I thought you said he was innocent. Yet you're chasing after him."

"Detective Frogert." Sadie's voice was even firmer than before. "I had no idea Luke Manning worked at Free Harvest until I got there this morning. And I still think he's innocent, more so now than before, in fact."

"How so?"

"I took a box of truffles from next door as a donation to the food bank," Sadie said. "He clearly saw the logo and didn't react any differently than when I asked him about fishing." Just verbalizing this bothered Sadie as it caused her to think back to the "favor" she had done for Froggy. Even though it had worked to her advantage, she never should have let Froggy goad her into that appointment at Manning Property Holdings.

"So you didn't go to check on Luke Manning this morning," Frogert conceded. "Maybe you suspected some of the other suspects would be there then?"

Sadie couldn't deny it so chose to say nothing at all.

"I believe I had asked you to back off, yet you continue to pursue this," Frogert said. He glanced at the plastic-covered note, apparently realizing his poor choice of words. "In order to let us do our job, that is."

Sadie wasn't sure how to respond. It seemed he was hindering her investigation more than she was hindering his. Then again, she wasn't the one officially assigned to the case, so he had a point.

"I'll call you later if we find anything out." Frogert left abruptly, clearly irritated with her lack of response.

"Great," Sadie said to the empty room.

TWENTY-THREE

Sadie looked at her watch, anticipating Amber's return at any moment. Business had been brisk since Amber left for her lunch date with Dylan but not more than she could handle on her own. The activity kept her mind off the troublesome note, not to mention Froggy's annoying visit. Plus Matteo sent over a new batch of samples in order to encourage customers to head over to his shop after leaving Flair. It seemed to be a good day in general. Aside from that pesky little detail of threats, of course, like the one left on her door that morning.

Amber was all smiles when she returned from lunch. Her rosy cheeks complemented her pink turtleneck perfectly, and the single red rose she held seemed to accentuate the glow. Coco, seeing Amber return, stood up from the counter pillow and sniffed the rose. Amber gave the petite canine a pat on the head.

"A successful outing, I take it?" Sadie fought to keep a teasing tone out of her voice. She knew Amber had been nervous enough. There was no reason to make it harder for her. Still, she was eager for a report. "Do tell."

"I'd say it was very successful," Amber said, blushing as she lifted a floating heart necklace off her turtleneck to show Sadie. "And we're going out again this coming weekend. A movie, I think, at least that's the tentative plan. And dinner."

"Dinner and a movie—perfect," Sadie said. She was happy

for Amber yet surprised to feel a wave of envy pass through her. The idea of dinner and a movie with Broussard sounded wonderful but impossible with the distance between them. Should she plan a return visit to New Orleans? Or maybe invite him to visit her in San Francisco? Both ideas seemed too forward. This was one of the problems with the distance. It was impossible to plan something little. The logistics alone made something simple into much more.

"Sadie?"

Amber's voice snapped her out of her reverie, and she realized her assistant had been speaking to her.

"I'm sorry, Amber," Sadie said. "My mind was somewhere else. What were you saying?"

"I was asking if Froggy had any ideas about that note on the door this morning. I'm worried you might be in trouble." Amber lowered her voice to a whisper as a female customer approached the counter. The woman sampled a truffle, picked up a bottle of hand lotion as if intending to buy it, put the bottle back down, sampled another truffle, and walked away.

"He's going to check it for prints," Sadie said. "Who knows if he'll find anything or not."

Amber's rosy glow paled. "My prints might be on it, though I did try to only touch the tape when I took it off the door."

Sadie smiled. "Don't worry. He knows you were the one to find it on the door. Besides, neither one of us would have a reason to leave the note."

"Speaking of which," Amber said. "Who would?"

"That's the question of the day, I'd say." Sadie sighed. "Anyone who didn't want to be found out, which could either be the killer or someone with something to hide. In this case, it seems everyone involved has something to hide, whether guilt over murder or guilt over infidelity. There are a lot of secrets buried in this maze of personalities."

"Perhaps you need to consult with a different detective," Amber suggested, a twinkle in her eye. "You know, for another opinion."

"Not a bad suggestion," Sadie said. "And it's a good excuse to call him. There's just one problem with that."

"I know. I know," Amber said. "He'll worry."

"Exactly." Sadie mulled this over. She could use Broussard's opinion but knew it would come with a well-meaning lecture. On the other hand, it seemed Broussard and Froggy were in contact with each other over this case, so maybe Broussard was going to find out about it anyway. Better to have it come directly from her.

Taking advantage of a lull in store activity, Sadie took Coco and escaped to the back. Setting Coco down on the floor, she retrieved her cell phone from the desk and contemplated sending Broussard a text. She paced back and forth, a movement Coco insisted on mimicking. Finally she settled into her desk chair and typed out a text.

Detective Broussard.

Not getting an immediate answer, she set the phone down faceup and tapped her fingers on the desktop. Now that she'd gathered the nerve to discuss updated events with him, she was anxious. Fortunately she didn't have to wait long.

Ms. Kramer.

Ah, there he was. Close by in terms of technology but not close enough to lecture her for her continued involvement. Dinner and movie aside, this felt like the best situation at the moment. She weighed a few options and then sent back a text.

A few new developments here. Need your opinion.

There, that wasn't so hard, Sadie thought. A simple

statement of fact, followed by a kind request for help from a friend.

Like the note on your door this morning?

Well. She wasn't expecting that. So much for easing into the conversation.

You've talked to Froggy, she typed. Obviously it wasn't even a question.

Call me. No, I'll call.

Sadie watched the screen light up with the incoming call. It was tempting to answer, just to hear his voice. But while her office was relatively private, it was still just a few feet away from the back of the store. In addition, her office and the dressing room shared a wall. She waited until the call stopped and then typed another text.

At the store. Not private enough.

Sadie watched the little dots on the screen that indicated he was typing a response.

Good call. Frogert asked if I knew anyone who might be trying to threaten you.

That made sense, not because Broussard was a detective but simply because he knew her. Of course Froggy would contact him. He probably checked with Matteo and Amber as well. She made a mental note to follow up with both of them.

What did you say? I mean, what do you think? Suddenly befuddled, Sadie wasn't quite sure what she meant to ask. She didn't really care what he had told Froggy when it came down to it. She just wondered what Broussard's own take on it was.

Six possibilities.

Sadie nodded.

Three men, three women.

She nodded again.

Are you there?

Sorry, Sadie typed. *I was just nodding, agreeing with you.*

Well, I can't see you from here.

Sadie smiled, appreciating their mutual affinity for dry humor.

Look at the possible motives, Broussard sent.

Motives? Sadie returned, hoping for more clarification.

I'm being paged. Please call me later, Broussard typed.

Will do. Sadie sent the short reply knowing he was already off and running.

Motives… Sadie sat back in her chair. Motives for the murder? Or motives for leaving the note? They were not the same thing. But somehow they were linked. That was what she needed to figure out, why each of the suspects might have left the note. That might just lead to the answer to the bigger question: Who killed Sue Bennett?

TWENTY-FOUR

Considering the question of motives, Sadie decided a bit of fortification was in order. After checking with Amber to make sure everything was fine, she headed over to Matteo's. As expected, the place was swamped with last-minute holiday purchases. She helped herself to a sample raspberry-espresso truffle and took a seat at one of several ice-cream-shop-style tables.

It was a lot to ponder, the inner workings of six different people's minds. As for the murder itself, jealousy seemed the obvious choice. It certainly was for the women—and maybe even for the men, if they'd found out about each other. There was always a chance of that "if I can't have her, then no one can" type of thinking.

Luke Manning? She'd definitely ruled him out. He was far too casual in his reactions to both the fishing comments and the Cioccolato logo. In addition, she was starting to wonder if he'd even been seeing Sue Bennett on anything other than a professional basis. It had sounded like he wasn't even the one who'd ordered the Valentine's chocolates. Apparently his fiancée ordered gifts for his clients. Or did his receptionist? Ah, there was something she never would have considered if he hadn't mentioned the fact he didn't order his own gifts.

Sadie sighed and turned her thoughts to Bruno. Of the three men the victim had been seeing—if in fact she *was* seeing them all—Bruno struck her as the roughest. He was definitely the gruffest of them all, and she was certain he was the strongest physically. Would that make him more able to strangle someone? Or did that particular method of murder have nothing to do with strength? It wasn't like *she* had any personal experience with this.

Zane of Zany Z's was hard to read. He didn't seem like the type to get overly jealous. With all the women he'd had hanging around him at the bar, Sadie was pretty sure his modus operandi was that of a player, more interested in the women being interested in *him* than the other way around. She suspected Sue was only one of numerous flings Zane had. It's possible that finding out she was seeing someone else might not matter to him at all.

But it *could* matter to Lila.

That brought Sadie right around to the second set of suspects: the women. Like the saying went, *hell hath no fury like a woman scorned.* And Lila didn't hit Sadie as the type to shrink back and not stand up for herself. She'd be likely to suspect Zane too, based on his demeanor at the bar. Maybe she decided she'd put up with his wandering ways long enough and wanted to do something about it.

Gina, Bruno's counterpart, definitely seemed like the jealous type. The icy stare Sadie had received the first time she'd stopped by the crab shack still lingered in her memory. If Gina wasn't comfortable with Bruno conversing with female customers, she could only imagine the woman's reaction to finding out about an affair. Then again, she might be more likely to kill *him* than the woman involved. They did have those mallets handy after all.

And then there was Luke Manning's fiancée, whatever the elegant woman's name was. *Giselle? Isabella?* Maybe she suspected the chocolates were more than just a client gift.

Or that she should have been the recipient, not the client. This woman was the most mysterious of them all. All Sadie really knew about her was that she dressed well—overdressed was more like it—and that she knew the other two women since she'd seen the three of them together at Fisherman's Wharf. She knew the fiancée had been to Flair, if only to browse. That was it. She didn't even know the woman's name. Sadie almost wanted her to end up being the killer for the mystery of it all.

Sadie sighed and stood to allow other customers to have the table. Six suspects, multiple motives, and most still in the running. In fact, she reminded herself, she shouldn't entirely rule out Luke Manning. Maybe he was a brilliant actor. Maybe he knew Sadie was involved, suspected her trip to his office wasn't what it appeared to be. Maybe *he* had left the note on the door. Could Sue Bennett have been a disgruntled client who had uncovered some secret that would ruin his business? And he felt he had no choice but to do away with her?

No more late-night detective shows! Sadie thought to herself. She was heading into motive mania. Instead of broadening the scope at this point, she needed to narrow it down. She would hold to ruling Luke Manning out and concentrate on the others.

Returning to Flair—yes, of course she grabbed a truffle on the way—she helped Amber gift wrap a charm bracelet and then retired to her office to check her phone for messages. So deep in thought about the suspects' motives, she hadn't thought to take her phone with her to Matteo's. As it was, a text from Broussard waited on the screen.

No match for prints.

Well, Sadie thought. That was certainly fast. In addition, speaking of fast, she wasn't sure whether to be thrilled or worried that Froggy and Broussard seemed to have an instant connection on developments.

Already? It seemed the logical response. After all, Froggy had only left the shop a short while ago. How could they possibly know if there was a match for prints or not?

No prints. Broussard typed back.

Oh, right… It doesn't take any time to match prints if there aren't any to match.

Wiped clean? She typed back and then waited for a reply.

Have you thought of trying HGTV?

She could picture Broussard laughing, which really wasn't fair. It didn't take Columbo to imagine someone would wipe a note clean in order to not leave prints. In fact, she decided to tell Broussard exactly that.

It doesn't take Columbo to think someone would wipe a note like that clean. Sadie sighed as soon as she sent the text. Talk about proving her love of detective shows.

But do you wear a trench coat?

Ah, as she suspected, Broussard was familiar with the popular TV detective. After all, the show ran for decades.

Another text came in from Broussard before she could reply.

Let Frogert handle it. The note might not have been serious.

He did have a point there. The cutout magazine letters seemed a bit dramatic.

True, Sadie typed. *But it still means I'm involved.* Whether I want to be or not, she added silently. All this just because she tried to deliver chocolate and a nosy neighbor reported her car's license plate number. It was amazing how a simple errand could end up so convoluted.

Unfortunately, Broussard sent back.

I think it will be solved tonight. Sadie knew this might be too much information to give Broussard, but she sent the text anyway.

Why?

Volunteering at the food bank. Best to be a little vague, Sadie thought. No reason to point out she thought the suspects might all be there. *I'm giving them a donation of truffles.* It wasn't a lie. She was giving them the truffles. The fact she'd already dropped them off and was going back for other reasons was just a minor detail.

If truffles crack the case, let me know. We can add that to our crime-solving methods here in New Orleans.

Sadie laughed. *You may have to use beignets,* she typed back.

Whatever it takes.

That was exactly what Sadie had in mind. If her hunch was right, all the suspects would be at the food bank that evening. And if it took a box of truffles to give her an excuse to be there too, so be it. She stood up, preparing to help Amber close up shop.

Did Matteo give you anything besides the box of truffles?

Sadie laughed. Didn't the entire world understand how important truffles were?

A box of truffles that would retail for a few hundred dollars is enough of a donation.

Excellent point, Broussard texted back. *Let me know how it goes.*

Report to follow, Sadie answered dutifully.

The text exchange over, she put her cell phone away and helped close up the shop. After sending Coco off with Amber for a dog-sitting session, Sadie headed out.

TWENTY-FIVE

Before even entering Free Harvest, Sadie knew two of her suspects had already arrived. A somewhat dilapidated white van sat outside the entrance, the name BRUNO'S spelled out on the side in peeling paint. A salty, fishy smell wafted from the open rear doors of the vehicle as both "Brownie" and Gina unloaded crates of food, some labeled from other wharf businesses. Setting aside the fact that the two were murder suspects, Sadie admired the couple's kind nature in rounding up food from other vendors to deliver to the food bank.

Stepping inside the building, Sadie noted the dining room looked even more festive than it had that morning. Helium-filled red and white balloons hovered above chairs, tied at periodic intervals. Heart-shaped confetti dotted the tops of the tables, adding to the décor of streamers and construction paper left from earlier in the day.

Sadie was impressed. The community of volunteers had certainly come together to make this a special event for those attending. Even a few musicians from a local college had set up instruments in one corner of the room, planning to add to the ambiance of the evening. It seemed all the bases had been covered, not the least of which was the food.

"Glad you could make it!" Nora greeted her with enthusiasm, though she did glance down at Sadie's tote bag suspiciously, which hung from one of Sadie's elbows. Laughing, Sadie set down a second bag of goods she'd picked up at a market on the way over. With both hands, she opened her tote as if going through a security check. Nora nodded and grinned after looking inside and finding it free of potential canine mischief.

"It's the least I could do after the ruckus this morning," Sadie said.

"Don't even worry about it." Nora waved her hand in the air as if dismissing the memory. "Our regulars haven't had that much entertainment since Sid Samuel's toupee fell into his chicken noodle soup."

"Oh my," Sadie exclaimed.

"Yep. It was especially entertaining after he'd put it back on. You should have seen those noodles hanging down." Nora lifted her arms high and draped her fingers over her forehead. "Don't worry; he had more fun laughing than anyone else."

Sadie looked around at the tables again, imagining the variety of scenes the place saw during the course of the year. Eager diners already occupied many of the seats. She recognized Harold from breakfast that morning, which reminded her of the heavy bag she'd set on the floor. She picked it up and handed it to Nora.

"Thank you!" Nora exclaimed as she looked inside. "This many cans of orange juice concentrate will cover us for several mornings. You must have cleaned out the store's case!"

"Not quite. I did leave a few cans for other shoppers."

"Follow me," Nora said. "We'll put them in the freezer." She headed for the door to the back area, Sadie right behind her.

The scene in the kitchen was what she had pictured with one exception: the massive spread of food. Bowls of fresh green salad, baskets of dinner rolls, and foil-covered, ready-to-serve aluminum pans crowded ninety percent of the prep table. In one corner, Bruno was filling iced bins with fresh crab.

Another vendor entered and placed a heavy kettle on one of the few spots still open on the counter. He left and returned with one more. "Chili," he announced.

"Thanks, Tom," Nora said. "You know everyone loves your chili."

"Wow," Sadie said, looking around. A particularly appealing chocolate sheet cake caught her attention. *I simply have to hang out here more often.*

"Valentine's Day is our biggest event, believe it or not," Nora said. "So we receive generous donations from restaurants in the area. Private donors too."

"It's really your biggest?" Sadie said. "Even bigger than Thanksgiving or Christmas?"

"Definitely," Nora said. "Many places offer hearty meals for those holidays, but not many make Valentine's Day a special event. People get lonely around this time. There's so much emphasis on romance, happy couples, sweet greeting cards intended for a loved one—that sort of thing. Free Harvest gives them a place to be with others if single or widowed or without family."

A now-familiar voice pitched in. "Of course, couples are welcome too." Luke Manning smiled as he pulled a baked ham out of an oven, handing it to none other than his fiancée, who set it on a cutting board. As Sadie expected, it was the elegant woman she'd seen at his office, in her boutique, and with the other two women at the wharf.

What the heck is her name? Bound and determined to find out once and for all, she marched over and extended her arm toward the woman, who reached out and clasped it with a greasy plastic glove. "I'm Sadie Kramer." She regretted reaching for the ham-glazed hand but had the good manners to not yank it away.

"Gertrude Prunella Pigsby," the woman said. "But everyone calls me Gerp."

Sadie blinked. Quickly Nora sent her a nod to let her know it really was the woman's name. "Okay, Gerp it is," Sadie said. "Glad to meet you." *So much for Juliette, Anastasia, Giselle, or Isabella...*

"Lila should be here any minute," Nora said. "We'll move all this to the serving area then. We're just keeping everything warm for now."

Right on cue, Lila popped into the kitchen. Sadie watched the door, hoping... Yes, there he was, the sleazy boyfriend himself, a giant plastic bag of salty pretzel mix slung over his shoulder.

Sadie looked around and smiled. *They're all here. Perfect.*

TWENTY-SIX

S adie looked at the spread on the serving table, impressed. She'd been to wedding receptions with lesser fare. Honey-glazed ham, mashed potatoes, at least four varieties of salads, chili, and a gigantic basket of sourdough dinner rolls were only the start of the delicious offerings. An iced bin of cracked crab gave people the option of enjoying San Francisco's famed Dungeness crustacean. A Chinatown bakery had sent over miniature custard tarts. And of course, there was the chocolate sheet cake she had eyed in the kitchen. When Sadie found out it was a donation from Ghirardelli, she almost forgot why she came to the Valentine's Day dinner altogether.

Matteo's truffles, arranged beautifully around the cake, brought her back to reality. After all, bringing those as a donation had originally served as her ticket into what she suspected would be a showdown. It was unlikely all the suspects could be gathered together without something blowing up. And when Frogert showed up—which didn't surprise Sadie in the least—she knew she was right.

The band started into a rendition of "That's Amore," and guests fell into line as Nora, Luke, Lila, Sadie, and other volunteers juggled serving spoons, ladles, tongs, and cake knives to transfer food onto plates held in eager hands. Even after filling a good two hundred plates, there was plenty left. Musical selections moved through several love songs, keeping an even balance between songs applicable to singles as well as couples.

"I wish Sue could have been here," Luke said after the line dwindled down, his voice barely a whisper, as if talking to himself. However, it became apparent immediately that his comment was louder than he intended it to be.

"I'll bet you do," Gerp said. She smacked a scoop of mashed potatoes down on a guest's plate with such emphasis that the plate almost fell. She turned to eye Zane and Bruno next. "That goes for all three of you."

Luke opened his mouth to respond, but Zane replied first, looking at the women in an oddly calm manner that spoke more of curiosity than discomfort. "You all knew?" His statement was followed by mixed expressions on the other men's faces. Bruno paled while Luke merely looked confused.

"Get real," Lila said. "Of course we knew. She eyed all three men. I don't know why guys always think they can get away with that kind of stuff."

"But I…" Luke started to speak but was quickly drowned out by louder voices.

"Face it, Gina," Gerp said. "It was your idea from the beginning, a way to solve three problems at once."

Aha, Sadie thought. *Just as I suspected, they all planned the murder together. But it didn't go down that way, hence the argument at the wharf.*

"Gina's the one who insisted we call it off," Lila said.

"Well, that's true," Gerp admitted.

"Thank you, Lila," Gina said. She plastered on a grateful smile.

"You're welcome," Lila said politely.

Gina's smile quickly changed to a snide grin. "Which is why you must have done it."

Lila's mouth dropped open. "You know I never agreed with

the crazy idea from the start! I thought you guys were kidding around. We were all mad at her, but murder? A little extreme, don't you think?" Her gaze moved from one person to the next, finally landing on Detective Frogert.

"Seems extreme to me," Frogert said. Sadie, now standing next to the detective, almost burst out laughing.

Gerp spoke up, glaring at Lila. "Face it, Lila, you're the one who did it. You might as well admit it. You thought that boyfriend of yours was going to leave you for her."

"Zany? Ha! He'd never leave me." Lila examined her nails nonchalantly.

"How can you say that? He was cheating on you!" Gina pointed out.

Lila laughed. "Are you kidding me? He's done that a million times. I don't take it seriously anymore. I just feel sorry for the women, knowing he'll dump them and move on to someone new when he gets bored. Besides, he always comes back to me." She turned to Zane. "Isn't that right, sweetie?"

Zane had just grabbed a truffle, tossed it in the air, and caught it in his mouth. He swallowed and smiled. "That's right, honey bunch."

"It was you, Gerp," Lila said, "you and your highfalutin lifestyle. You knew if Luke left you for Sue that you'd lose that fortune you were about to marry into."

"What the…," Luke said, his voice trailing off.

"Are you calling me a gold digger?" Gerp shouted. "How dare you!" To Lila's shock and Zane's amusement, Gerp picked up a custard tart and smashed it into Lila's face.

Sadie noted several guests at tables had turned their chairs to face the front and were pointing and discussing the escalating activity. One person held up a cell phone horizontally with two hands.

"We have a prenup, you idiot!" Gerp shouted. "Why would I kill her? I had nothing to gain by her being out of the picture."

One motive bites the dust, Sadie thought to herself.

Lila, who had wiped the custard and crust off her face, grabbed a crab claw from the ice bin and poked Gerp's chest with it. Bruno frowned.

"Doesn't. Rule. Out. Jealousy," Lila said, one crabby poke per word.

"This is imported silk!" Gerp screamed.

A practical wardrobe item for a food bank indeed.

Frogert leaned toward Sadie. "Five bucks says it's Lila."

"You're on," Sadie said.

Luke cleared his throat and interrupted. "She was just a client."

"Stay out of it!" Both Gerp and Lila shouted together.

Wide-eyed, Luke looked at Zane, who shrugged his shoulders, another truffle halfway into his mouth. Both men looked at Bruno, who hovered over the ice bin, guarding the rest of the cracked crab with both hands. He didn't respond, seemingly determined to stay neutral. Or was his lack of involvement caused by nerves?

Sadie smiled as the band launched into a rendition of Frank Sinatra's "It Had to Be You." A floor show didn't get much better than this.

Keeping a close eye on Bruno, Sadie moved over by the ice bin. Giving her the same evil eye as she had the first time Sadie visited the crab stand, Gina moved possessively closer. Bruno stepped away from them both and began wringing his hands. Frogert, noting the behavior, began to move toward Bruno, which caused him to crack.

"I did it! I killed her!" Bruno shouted, drawing chatter from the crowd. The band stopped playing, if only to not miss out on the action.

Gina spun to face Bruno. "What?" She gasped as she saw Frogert reach into his back pocket for handcuffs. "No!" she shouted.

"*Zitta!*" Bruno yelled at Gina, "*Non dire nulla!*"

Be quiet! Don't say anything! Sadie was grateful for Italian lessons, though her intention had always been to use it for shopping in Rome, not for solving crimes.

"Just as I thought," Sadie said. "You can hold off on the handcuffs for a minute, Froggy."

Oops.

"Why? Wait… what did you call me?" Frogert kept a grip on Bruno's arm.

"Oh," Sadie said, quickly covering her tracks. "I said Frogert, but I meant to say *Detective* Frogert. Sorry. No offense."

"None taken," Frogert said, apparently accepting the explanation.

"Bruno, no!" Gina screamed again.

Sadie turned to Gina. "Are you going to let him go to prison for you?"

"*Non dire nulla!*" Bruno repeated, his eyes wild.

Lila stepped closer, her expression shocked. "Gina?"

Gerp approached right behind Lila. "You were the one who said it was a bad idea." Quickly she turned to the detective and added, "We were just kidding around anyway."

"Of course," Frogert said.

Gina collapsed into a chair. "It *was* a bad idea! That's why I went to her house."

Frogert released his hold on Bruno's arm. Bruno looked down and put his hands over his face. A hush came over the room. Even Zane looked serious.

"I just went to talk some sense into her," Gina said. "You know, to get her to stay away from them all." Lila and Gerp nodded, appreciating Gina's efforts in spite of being shocked.

"Continue," Frogert said.

"I only meant to confront her," Gina explained. "She had no right being a mistress!"

"Client," Luke muttered.

"It turned into an argument, and that's when I saw the card on her mantle," Gina said.

"The card?" Frogert moved closer to Gina, handcuffs ready.

"You are my favorite fruit of the sea!" Gina shouted. She stood and rushed to Bruno, grabbing the front of his shirt with both hands. "That's what you've always told me. That *I'm* your favorite fruit of the sea! How could you tell her the same thing? After all our years together! Bruno, how could you?"

"So what happened then?" Frogert coaxed.

"I saw that crab net in the corner of her living room," Gina continued. "I was so angry! I just wanted her out of our lives. I grabbed the rope from the net and…" She collapsed back into the seat, sobbing. Bruno put his arms around her, but she pushed him away.

Bruno turned to Sadie, devastated. "I tried to get you to back off!"

Sadie and Frogert exchanged looks. So *he* put the note on her door, trying to save Gina.

"Let's continue this down at the station." Frogert handcuffed Gina and led her out, leaving a stunned group of volunteers and diners behind.

Gerp moved to Luke's side and wrapped an arm around his waist, an apologetic gesture for doubting him. Lila and Nora attended to the buffet. Zane gave her a thumbs-up and went off to help. The band launched into "Unforgettable." Indeed, it was a Valentine's Day dinner that no one was likely to forget.

Sadie looked around and said the only thing that came to mind.

"Truffles, anyone?"

TWENTY-SEVEN

"Well, take a look at those!" Amber exclaimed as Sadie entered the shop. The arrangement of two dozen red roses looked just as beautiful as it had the evening before when Sadie had found it on her living room table along with a heart-shaped box of Matteo's fancy truffles.

Sadie laughed. "As if you haven't already seen them. You're the only one who has a key to my place."

"Point taken," Amber said. "They were delivered right after we closed up yesterday. You'd already headed out to the dinner. I figured they'd be a nice surprise when you got home, so I didn't text you. It took willpower to not tell you about them when you picked up Coco."

"They were a fabulous surprise," Sadie said. "It was very sweet of Broussard to send them. I called and thanked him immediately." She set the vase of flowers toward the end of the sale counter where customers could enjoy them and then helped Coco get settled on her pillow.

"Have you recovered from last night?" Amber asked.

"Barely," Sadie admitted. "I stayed to help package up extra food to send home. Many of the guests said it was... Let me see if I can remember some of the comments... 'better than the latest mystery read,' 'a unique experience,' and my personal favorite, 'funnier than *Saturday Night Live.*' Oh, and one person requested an encore next year."

"Good luck pulling that off," Amber said.

"Indeed," Sadie agreed. "That was one wild Valentine's Day. Not quite sure how we'd top it. Full of mystery and romance. And speaking of romance…"

A chime signaled the arrival of a customer, a woman in her fifties with a tote bag similar to Sadie's. She headed to the sale rack to browse discounted selections. Amber smiled as Dylan entered just behind her, his arms empty.

"No UPS deliveries today?" Sadie said, smiling.

"Just one," Dylan said. He leaned across the counter and gave Amber a sweet kiss.

"I need to thank Matteo for setting aside that Valentine's Day truffle assortment for Broussard's order," Sadie said, heading for the front door. "Be right back." With only one customer, it was a good time to run next door. And it would give Amber and Dylan a chance to flirt for a few minutes without her hovering over them. She knew Amber would keep an eye on the woman in case she needed help.

Cioccolato was quiet, almost empty, as Sadie knew it would be on a postholiday morning. Half of San Francisco was likely to be on a sugar high for a week just from the amount of business Matteo had done over the past few days.

Matteo looked up from a tray of pecan turtles and smiled as Sadie entered.

"Just wanted to thank you for the box of truffles," Sadie said.

"Well, they weren't from me, you know." Matteo winked at her. "You have a not-so-secret admirer, you know. By the way, he wanted me to make sure it was an assortment of your favorites. Very nice."

"And what did you tell him?" Sadie said.

"I told him the truth," Matteo said. "They're all your favorites."

"Absolutely," Sadie said. "I'm an equal opportunity chocolate aficionado."

"I heard you cracked the Sue Bennett case last night," Matteo said.

Sadie raised an eyebrow. "You did? Where did you hear that?"

"Over in that back corner," Matteo said, nodding toward the back of the shop.

Sadie turned, surprised to see Froggy enjoying a café mocha with the morning newspaper.

"I was on my way over to your store to thank you," Frogert said. "Couldn't resist a little detour in here first."

"Thank me?" Sadie said. "I figured you thought I've been in your way the past few days."

Frogert nodded. "That too, of course." He managed a slight smile. "But I wouldn't have thought to connect everyone to Free Harvest without your help."

"Or the amateur crabbing club?"

"No, I knew about that," Frogert said. "That was the connection between Sue Bennett and the men. But I didn't see the link between the women. Obviously, they had to know each other from somewhere…"

"…in order to figure out that the guys all knew the same woman, Sue Bennett." Sadie finished the sentence for him.

"But how did *they* figure it out?" Frogert took one more gulp of his coffee and stood up, folding his newspaper under his arm.

Sadie almost laughed. For a detective, Froggy was a tad slow on this point. Then again, he was not looking at it from a female viewpoint. "By comparing notes." Sadie smiled. *Never underestimate the power of women's intuition.* "So, Gina and Bruno?"

"Both in a lot of trouble," Frogert said. "Obviously, murder is murder. But covering it up is also a crime."

Sadie nodded. As for Lila and Gerp—*seriously, Gerp?*—Sadie didn't need to ask if anything would happen to them. Maybe they'd originally conspired to commit murder; maybe they only joked about it. There was no way to know.

"Thank you, Detective Frogert," Sadie said, shaking the detective's hand.

"Thank you," Frogert replied. "And thank that Broussard friend of yours for his help."

"For trying to keep me out of your way part of the time?" Sadie asked

"Your words, not mine," Frogert said. He tipped an imaginary hat and left.

Sadie returned to Flair as Dylan was heading out the door. She found Amber still blushing from the young man's visit as she rang up a purchase for the woman. Coco sniffed at the woman's tote bag when she set it on the counter to take out her wallet.

Nudging Coco, Sadie whispered, "Coco, be polite." She then complimented the customer on the petite nautical-print bandana she was purchasing, suggesting it might work as a scarf for her neck, maybe with a crisp white blouse in the summertime. Again she nudged Coco away from the woman's bag.

"Oh, it's not for me," the woman said. "It's for..." She looked down at Coco and then back up at Sadie. "Well, you seem to be pet friendly here, so..." Reaching into her tote, she pulled out a Yorkie almost identical in size to Coco, with slightly darker fur. "It's for Winston here. He just loves a little *flair*." She tied the bandana loosely around the dog's neck. The Yorkie stood tall, proudly modeling the new accessory.

"I couldn't have said it better myself," Sadie exclaimed. "It's perfect!" Apparently, Sadie wasn't the only one who thought so, as Coco trotted right over to Winston. After a few sniffs, the two Yorkies sat down side by side.

Amber handed the customer a receipt and thanked her for her purchase. Sadie was certain Coco and Winston leaned toward each other as the woman put Winston back in her bag and left the shop.

"Not a bad Valentine's Day," Sadie said as she leaned over the roses and breathed in their sweet scent.

"Murder aside," Amber said.

"Yes," Sadie agreed. "Murder aside."

Amber smiled and fingered the necklace Dylan had given her.

Coco simply yipped and stared at the front door.

"I think this calls for two truffles and one dog bone, don't you think, girls?" Sadie pulled a few treats from a drawer under the counter and doled them out appropriately.

"Absolutely," Amber said.

"To Valentine's Day." Sadie offered a mock toast with her truffle in one hand and the dog bone in the other. Amber reciprocated by lifting her own truffle in the air. Coco took the treat eagerly from Sadie.

Yes, Sadie thought as she bit into the melt-in-your-mouth chocolate. *Not a bad Valentine's Day at all.*

Spicy Chocolate Truffles

(Submitted by Kim Davis, from her blog, Cinnamon and Sugar and a Little Bit of Murder)

Ingredients

Truffles:
- 1 14-ounce sweetened condensed milk
- 16 ounces good-quality bittersweet chocolate chips or bars chopped into small pieces
- 2 teaspoons vanilla extract
- 1 teaspoon ground cinnamon
- 1/4 - 1/2 teaspoon cayenne powder, depending on how spicy you like it
- 1/4 teaspoon sea salt

Garnish:
- Your choice of cocoa powder, hot cocoa mix, nonmelting confectioners' sugar, or holiday-themed candy sprinkles

Instructions

For the truffles:
1. Heat the sweetened condensed milk in a small saucepan just until the edges start to bubble. Don't bring to a boil.
2. Place the chocolate in a medium-sized, heat-proof bowl. Pour the hot milk over the chocolate and allow to sit for two minutes. Add the vanilla, sea salt, cinnamon, and cayenne powder and stir until the chocolate is fully melted.
3. Cover and refrigerate until chilled, around 1 hour.
4. Roll the chilled mixture into small balls, and then roll into your choice of garnish.
5. Serve truffles at room temperature. Store leftovers in the refrigerator.

Acknowledgements

Sadie and Coco's Valentine adventure only came together with the help of others, as well as a few doses of chocolate!

I owe tremendous thanks to Annie Sarac at The Editing Pen for polishing up A Flair for Truffles as well as putting up with my overuse of commas. Keri Knutson of Alchemy Book Covers and Design deserves praise for the wonderful covers that grace the Sadie Kramer Flair Mysteries. Formatting credit goes to Tara Meyers, who always manages to help me out when I'm in a time crunch. I'm fortunate to have top-notch insight from beta readers Jay Garner, Louise Martens, and Karen Putnam. Their feedback always makes these stories better. Special thanks go out to Charles Garner for his knowledge of fishing and crabbing procedures. And if there's such a thing as a beta listener, that praise goes to Paul Sterrett, who puts up with my daily verbal ramblings as I mull over plot points from the very first word to the last.

If you're experiencing a craving for chocolate after reading this story, you're in luck. Kim Davis has generously contributed the truffles recipe at the end of the book. You'll find directions for many more delicious goodies at her blog, Cinnamon and Sugar and a Little Bit of Murder.

Above all, I'm grateful for the support of my amazing family, friends, and readers. Their encouragement allows Sadie and Coco to find new adventures.

Books by Deborah Garner

The Paige MacKenzie Series

Above the Bridge

When NY reporter Paige MacKenzie arrives in Jackson Hole, it's not long before her instincts tell her there's more than a basic story to be found in the popular, northwestern Wyoming mountain area. A chance encounter with attractive cowboy Jake Norris soon has Paige chasing a legend of buried treasure passed down through generations. Side- stepping a few shady characters who are also searching for the same hidden reward, she will have to decide who is trustworthy and who is not.

The Moonglow Café

The discovery of an old diary inside the wall of the historic hotel soon sends NY reporter Paige MacKenzie into the underworld of art and deception. Each of the town's residents holds a key to untangling more than one long-buried secret, from the hippie chick owner of a new age café to the mute homeless man in the town park. As the worlds of western art and sapphire mining collide, Paige finds herself juggling research, romance, and danger.

Three Silver Doves

The New Mexico resort of Agua Encantada seems a perfect destination for reporter Paige MacKenzie to combine work with well-deserved rest and relaxation. But when suspicious jewelry shows up on another guest, and the town's storyteller goes missing, Paige's R&R is soon redefined as restlessness and risk. Will an unexpected overnight trip to Tierra Roja Casino lead her to the answers she seeks, or are darker secrets lurking along the way?

Hutchins Creek Cache

When a mysterious 1920's coin is discovered behind the Hutchins Creek Railroad Museum in Colorado, Paige MacKenzie starts digging into four generations of Hutchins family history, with a little help from the Denver Mint. As legends of steam engines and coin mintage mingle, will Paige discover the true origin of the coin, or will she find herself riding the rails dangerously close to more than one long-hidden town secret?

Crazy Fox Ranch

As Paige MacKenzie returns to Jackson Hole, she has only two things on her mind: enjoy life with Wyoming's breathtaking Grand Tetons as the backdrop, and spend more time with handsome cowboy Jake Norris as he prepares to open his guest ranch. But when a stranger's odd behavior leads her to research western filming in the area—in particular, the movie *Shane*, will it simply lead to a freelance article for the *Manhattan Post*, or will it lead to a dangerous hidden secret?

The Sadie Kramer Flair Series

A Flair for Chardonnay

When flamboyant senior sleuth Sadie Kramer learns the owner of her favorite chocolate shop is in trouble, she heads for the California wine country with a tote-bagged Yorkie and a slew of questions. The fourth-generation Tremiato Winery promises answers, but not before a dead body turns up at the vintners' scheduled Harvest Festival. As Sadie juggles truffles, tips, and turmoil, she'll need to sort the grapes from the wrath in order to find the identity of the killer.

A Flair for Drama

When a former schoolmate invites Sadie Kramer to a theatre production, she jumps at the excuse to visit the Monterey Bay area for a weekend. Plenty of action is expected on stage, but when the show's leading lady turns up dead, Sadie finds herself faced with more than one drama to follow. With both cast members and production crew as potential suspects, will Sadie and her sidekick Yorkie, Coco, be able to solve the case?

A Flair for Beignets

With fabulous music, exquisite cuisine, and rich culture, how could a week in New Orleans be anything less than fantastic for Sadie Kramer and her sidekick Yorkie, Coco? And it is... until a customer at a popular patisserie drops dead face-first in a raspberry-almond tart. A competitive bakery, a newly formed friendship, and even her hotel's luxurious accommodations offer possible suspects. As Sadie sorts through a gumbo of interconnected characters, will she discover who the killer is, or will the killer discover her first?

A Flair for Truffles

Sadie Kramer's friendly offer to deliver three boxes of gourmet Valentines truffles for her neighbor's chocolate shop backfires when she arrives to find the intended recipient deceased. Even more intriguing is the fact that the elegant heart-shaped gifts were ordered by three different men. With the help of one detective and the hindrance of another, Sadie will search San Francisco for clues. But will she find out "whodunit" before the killer finds a way to stop her?

A Flair for Flip-Flops

When the body of a heartthrob celebrity washes up on the beach outside Sadie Kramer's luxury hotel suite, her fun in the sun soon turns into sleuthing with the stars. The resort's wine and appetizer gatherings, suspicious guest behavior, and casual strolls along the beach boardwalk may provide clues, but will they be enough to discover who the killer is, or will mystery and mayhem leave a Hollywood scandal unsolved?

The Moonglow Christmas Series

Mistletoe at Moonglow

The small town of Timberton, Montana, hasn't been the same since resident chef and artist, Mist, arrived, bringing a unique new age flavor to the old western town. When guests check in for the holidays, they bring along worries, fears, and broken hearts, unaware that Mist has a way of working magic in people's lives. One thing is certain: no matter how cold winter's grip is on each guest, no one leaves Timberton without a warmer heart.

Silver Bells at Moonglow

Christmas brings an eclectic gathering of visitors and locals to the Timberton Hotel each year, guaranteeing an eventful season. Add in a hint of romance, and there's more than snow in the air around the small Montana town. When the last note of Christmas carols has faded away, the soft whisper of silver bells from the front door's wreath will usher guests and townsfolk back into the world with hope for the coming year.

Gingerbread at Moonglow

The Timberton Hotel boasts an ambiance of near-magical proportions during the Christmas season. As the aromas of ginger, cinnamon, nutmeg, and molasses mix with heartfelt camaraderie and sweet romance, holiday guests share reflections on family, friendship, and life. Will decorating the outside of a gingerbread house prove easier than deciding what goes inside?

Nutcracker Sweets at Moonglow

When a nearby theatre burns down just before Christmas, cast members of *The Nutcracker* arrive at the Timberton Hotel with only a sliver of holiday joy. Camaraderie, compassion, and shared inspiration combine to help at least one hidden dream come true. As with every Christmas season, this year's guests will face the New Year with a renewed sense of hope.

Snowfall at Moonglow

As holiday guests arrive at the Timberton Hotel with hopes of a white Christmas, unseasonably warm weather hints at a less-than-wintery wonderland. But whether the snow falls or not, one thing is certain: with resident artist and chef, Mist, around, there's bound to be a little magic. No one ever leaves Timberton without renewed hope for the future.

Stand-alone: *Cranberry Bluff*

Molly Elliott's quiet life is disrupted when routine errands land her in the middle of a bank robbery. Accused and cleared of the crime, she flees both media attention and mysterious, threatening notes to run a bed and breakfast on the Northern California coast. Her new beginning is peaceful until five guests show up at the inn, each with a hidden agenda. As true motives become apparent, will Molly's past come back to haunt her, or will she finally be able to leave it behind?

For more information on Deborah Garner's books:
Facebook: https://www.facebook.com/deborahgarnerauthor
Twitter: https://twitter.com/PaigeandJake
Website: http://deborahgarner.com
Mailing list: http://bit.ly/deborahgarner